GIDI

BOER

by

MALCOLM COLLEY

Cover by: Lesley Scull
Model: Chris Lines

"The Americans fight for a free world, the English mostly for honour and glory and medals, the French and Canadians decide too late that they have to participate. The Italians are too scared to fight; the Russians have no choice. The Germans for the Fatherland. The Boers? .... Those sons of bitches fight for the hell of it." American General, George "Guts and Glory" Patton

Author's note –
I think the same was said of the Irish, as long as it is against the English.

AUTHORS NOTE

Please keep in mind that this is not meant to be a history lesson. Although the history parts are events that I have been told or may have read or may have been taught at school, they do rely on my memory. I do remember complaining at school that we were taught a lot of South African history and little else or so it seemed to us. I also grew up with the giants of South African story telling on my bedside table, especially true stories of the bush by the likes of T.V. Bulpin, Stuart Cloete, Robert Ruark, Laurens Van Der Post, E. Cronje Wilmot, H C Bosman and many more that I can't remember.

I believe that South African history has much in common with the American West. The clashes between the cultures of the white settlers and the indigenous population, the struggle with the wild

elements and animals and later with the British rule. Of course, there was the lawlessness, greed, hate and love of a country during its birth pangs and so there must be many stories to tell, this being one of many. Things of the bush, I am sure of. In my mind I can still feel the sand between my toes as I walked to school. I can still smell the approaching thunder-storm, the smell of the wet grass after the storm, the smell of a bush fire and the sounds of early evening in the bush on my walk home, as a teenager, from hunting for my mother's cooking pot.

I still go back to hear the bark of the baboon in the kloof and smell the dust kicked up by a heard of wildebeest on their way down to the water-hole. Anyway, enjoy the fiction, it may well have happened just as I have reported.

ACKNOWLEDGEMENTS

Again, a special thanks must go to my daughter Lesley without whose badgering, ruthless editing and support, my first book would never have been published, for her help in designing the covers and publishing. Continued thanks to my daughter Sharon and son Thomas for their continued motivation.

Thanks to Anne Rooke for editing this book.

Also by Malcolm Colley:

Zachariah: The Boer Diamond

Ignasius: The Boer Gold

Dorothea: The Boer Treasure

Jedidiah: The Boer Thunder

PROLOGUE

By 1902 the war was over. It has taken three years and 330,000 soldiers to hammer 30,000 Boer men and boys into submission. The British employed a scorched earth policy and removed the women and children on the farms to stop the Boer Commandoes from obtaining supplies. Also, with ammunition in short supply, the Boers signed the Treaty of Peace of Vereeninging on May31 1902. The Boers were forced to surrender their arms and sign a declaration of allegiance to the Queen. Paul Kruger, the Boer leader, left the country but prior to him leaving he attempted to negotiate a deal with Holland and Germany for arms and ammunition in exchange for gold. The arms and ammunition reached the port of Lorenco Marques but the gold, sent by Kruger, went missing. It never reached the port so the ships sailed for home. Into this chaos of the aftermath of the war with men, woman and children trying to make it back to the farms, Gideon Barron, an Irishman born in South Africa is accused of helping to steal the gold and hunted by his fellow Boers for treason. With the help of what becomes his friends, he attempts to prove his innocence. Travelling across, what was then, the Transvaal Republic they follow the path of the robbers Meanwhile the true robbers manage to get away with most of the gold, some travelling into the Portuguese Protectorate of Mozambique and some beyond but some gold is left behind due to a misunderstanding. This is just one of the many stories about the disappearance of the gold. According to many stories the gold never left South Africa. Some say the gold was worth £500,000 in the value of that time. Some say that there was no gold, that the boxes were filled with ammunition destined for the Boer Commandoes fighting on the front.

"Sir," Gideon replied, "if the Lord is with us,
why has all this happened to us?
And where are all the miracles our ancestors told
us about?"
Judges 6:13

CHAPTER 1

The eagle perched on the rock right at the top of the *kopje* and surveyed the horizon. It was the beginning of summer and, even this late in the evening, it was still hot. He was looking east and so had the setting sun at his back. He cocked his head left and right and then back again and ruffled his feathers.

The small dust cloud had been moving in his direction for a few hours now. With his excellent vision he could see that it was a man on a horse. The eagle cocked his head sideways. This man was sitting at an angle. The eagle had seen this way of sitting before and knew that this man wasn't going to reach this *kopje* before he fell off. He could see the blood. Blood caked the front of his shirt and had pooled and coagulated around his belt. Blood excited him and he watched with interest. He didn't eat humans nor did he eat dead animals but anything dying interested him.

The eagle dropped forward off the rock, dived for a few seconds and then opened his wings to catch the upward current to take him to five thousand feet. Not that he knew that it was five thousand feet but he knew what his ultimate hunting height was. He banked on the thermal and looked down on the rider. The rider was laying forward on the horse now. The horse came abreast of the farmhouse and cut away from his course west toward the farmyard. He had to move over the ploughed field, ploughed to take *mielies*. Of course, the *mielies* wouldn't get planted. It was already a bit late in the season and the woman was alone on the farm. She had been alone since the outbreak of the war. Her man had left to go fight and the labourers had left before the end of the winter. The woman had struggled to plough this one field, the eagle had watched her.

All the eagle was sorry about was that the *mielie* pits would not be sown. The eagle didn't eat *mielie* pits but nice juicy hares and rats did eat the pits. When the pits are sown, the hares come out just before dark. That is when the eagle could choose his evening meal. He would dive and, while the hare was busy with his corn, at the last second, the eagle would turn talons down. The hare would hear the rush of wind too late.

Anyway, as the horse walked into the farmyard, the woman came out of the house with a rifle in her hands but when the man fell sideways off the horse, she looked around before leaving the rifle on the *stoep* and ran toward him. He was too heavy for her to lift and she had no help on the farm anymore. Luckily, he wasn't altogether unconscious. She helped him to his feet and he leaned heavily on her. Together they staggered to the house.

As the eagle banked, he saw a larger dust cloud. Because of his excellent eyesight, he could see five riders, the front one leaning forward to look for spoor. The eagle looked back at the woman. She was sharp, she scuffed the area where the man had fallen off his horse, vaulted into the saddle and galloped the horse down to the stream to the west of the farmyard. Then she jumped off, pointed him downstream and slapped his rump.

Not that the eagle cared but he could see that she needed to hurry, those riders were coming fast.

She sat on the bench on the *stoep* with the rifle across her knees and waited. She didn't have long to wait. The chickens scattered with a squawk as the riders thundered into the yard. The eagle watched as she pointed down toward the stream. They pulled their horses around and jumped into a gallop but the eagle knew they would be back and the woman knew it too. As soon as they were out of sight, she ran to the shed at the side of the house and came out leading a big black stallion. No saddle because there was no time. She helped the man out of the house, onto the horse and vaulted, spread legged, up behind. She did however grab the man's bag on the way and her Mauser was slung across her back.

The big black whirled round and took off at a gallop. The eagle watched them tearing through the bush and watched the five men come back later, warily because they didn't know what to expect. When there was no gunfire, they dismounted and went into the house. At the same time the lean mean one was skirting the farmyard, looking for spoor. He picked it up with a shout as the others came out of the house. The eagle watched as they took off in the right direction but at least the couple had a head start. The house bloomed into flame behind them.

The woman stretched the stallion and flew. She knew this bush like the back of her hand, having hunted here with her father and brothers from the age of six. Her mother had insisted on the age of six, only she knew why. The horse virtually flew through the bush. She took the big black through a *kloof*, just wide enough to let him through without scraping their legs. She knew that staying ahead was only temporary.

There was a cave directly in front of the *kloof* but it was well hidden. There was a shallow stream that they crossed and then up the opposite bank to the cave. The horse's hooves echoed as he walked into the entrance but further back the floor was soft dirt. Her boots made a soft 'puff' sound as they hit the dirt. The man slid into her arms and then onto the floor because she wasn't strong enough to hold him. She knew she should check for snakes, she had found a puff-adder in here once before but right now, there was no time to do any looking around.

Leaving the man there for the moment, she turned her attention to the entrance and pulled a dry branch that she had used before, to help conceal the cave. The man had pulled himself into a sitting position against a wall so she concentrated on the narrow pass that they had come through. The hunters would soon be coming through and she was praying that they wouldn't see the tracks leading to the cave. The stream was a good diversion and it worked, as it had many times before when she had hidden while playing with her brothers

.

The men hesitated momentarily at the entrance to the *kloof*. They knew they were sitting ducks coming through one at a time and no cover for the length of the pass. But the girl didn't shoot, she knew they were safer staying hidden. She held her Mauser sights on each one of them as they came through. The men gathered at the stream and, just as her brothers had always done, they assumed that she had headed downstream.

The man and girl didn't speak as she slowly helped him out of his blood-soaked shirt. Some of the blood had dried into a hard board. He had taken two closely placed bullets just below the collar-bone but the girl didn't know that. Not dangerous in themselves but it was obvious that he had lost a lot of blood.

His face was ashen even through the deep tan from long hours of work in the sun. The blood had coagulated in the wound now but she would have to clean it to stop festering. She had herbs in her back-yard garden that her mother had brought up from the Karoo but they couldn't help her now. There was also buchu leaves and tea in her kitchen but might as well be a hundred miles away. She did know of a hollow tree trunk that had fallen over and where bees usually formed their hive, not too far but she would have to wait. The men would soon be back when they saw that the trail didn't leave the stream.

She glanced at the man to make sure he was alright and then left the cave and scrambled down to the water's edge, taking a bucket with her that she had left there before. The tracks were obvious to anyone taking a closer look. Taking a dry branch nearby, she swept the tracks away being careful to make it look natural. She was only halfway up the slope again with the bucket of water, when she heard the men coming back. Lying between two boulders she didn't dare to even peep at them. She had to listen and pray that they wouldn't come up this side of the stream.

The men milled around the entrance to the pass, in and out of the stream and both sides of the stream. Not finding any tracks, they single-filed through the *kloof*. These were hard men and not used to giving up. They retraced their steps slowly, searching both sides of their ride back to the house. The sun was gone now and it would soon be dark. The house was still burning. They circled the house to the barn. There were long leaves of tobacco hanging in the eaves and strips of *biltong* near the door. Chickens were roosting for the night so it was easy to slaughter a big rooster and whip some potatoes from the rack where they had been pulled and hung ready to be cleaned and taken in.

This was the best night they had spent since they had flushed the man they were hunting three days ago. They knew that they had put two bullets in him because they had seen him fall after the impact. How he had slipped away from them had amazed even these hard men. It hadn't taken them long to pick up his trail but now he had slipped away again, most certainly with the help of that girl. Why she would help a stranger, they didn't know. This was a thief who had stolen from the Boer cause. They had been sent to find him in the name of Paul Kruger and to find out where he and his helpers had hidden the gold. Gold that should have gone to buying arms and ammunition was now missing. It left a bitter taste in the mouth to think that a man would take away the only hope they had left of maybe inflicting harm on the British who were driving them from their homes and who had taken their women and children into concentration camps. The men were told to draw the information from him in any manner necessary.

The girl was sure the men wouldn't come back after dark. As soon as they disappeared through the pass, she climbed down taking the small bucket from the cave and followed the stream to the hollow log. This was the best time of day to take honey but she had to get back before total darkness. Not that she was scared of the bush at night but she didn't want to fall in the *kloof*. If she broke a leg now, they would both die.

The bees were settling in for the night and it was easy to take a few small slabs of honeycomb. Her brain was working in a frenzy and she forced herself to calm down. She scooped water from the stream. The jackals were calling to each other by the time she arrived back at the cave.

The man was unconscious or asleep when she walked in. She took a long look at him, not much to look at, big, about six foot six, not a lot of muscle but also no fat. His clothes had seen better days. His blood-soaked shirt had been thrown to one side. His trousers looked like British army but he was wearing *veldskoene*, typical Boer shoes.

It was safe to build the fire a bit higher, she needed some light. She gently washed the blood away and gingerly felt for the bullet. It was deep and would need a knife point to dig it out. Using the sleeves from the man's shirt, she bandaged the honey-comb onto the wound. The bullet would have to come out or lead poisoning would set in. She hesitated but then decided to wait for daylight. The only downside was that he would be awake and feel every movement that she made with the knife. She slept next to him on the bare sand. He moaned in the night and she lay a wet rag on his forehead.

The men came back at daybreak, through the pass. This time they climbed off their horses and slowly searched both sides of the stream. The girl lay in the mouth of the cave ready with her Mauser. The man was awake and she held her finger in front of her lips for him to be quiet. He was sweating; obviously in pain. She turned her attention back to the men outside.

The cave was well hidden and she thought of days gone by. Her name was Lorraine. Her family and friends called her Rainkies, not that she had many of either family or friends around lately. Her two brothers and father hadn't come back from the war yet and she had had no news of them. Her mother had died many years ago, of what she wasn't sure. The farm workers had left. She had encouraged them to leave when they heard that the British were taking the blacks, as well as the white women and children into so called concentration camps. The workers had all promised to come back once the war was over. Lorraine herself had gone to live in Pretoria until a month ago when the peace treaty was signed.

She watched the men over the sights of her rifle. They were baffled. They stood and talked and looked around. All of a sudden one gave a shout and pointed to the ground. The others ran over, looked at the ground and looked up toward the cave but it was too well hidden. They slowly turned away, all but the leader. He turned and sat on a log facing the cave.

Lorraine kept her sights on him. There was a very slight quiver in her left arm. She calmed her breathing. Shooting a man was not the same as shooting a buck but she hadn't even shot a buck since her fourteenth birthday. Her oldest brother, Willem, had taken her with him to shoot for the pot. That wasn't the first time they had hunted together. They were on foot and came across an Impala ram grazing. His head came up and they froze. Willem indicated with his eyes that she should take the shot. It took him in the neck instead of the head and the Impala dropped but not dead. They ran over to where the buck lay motionless but still alive. His eyes rolled when they got to him and the buck started crying with the same sound as a baby crying.
Willem looked at her staring at the wounded buck and put a second shot through its head. That sound had haunted her for a long time after and she had never shot another buck since then.

Now Lorraine was faced with a tougher choice. Not really a choice because she knew that if he moved up the slope, she would have to kill more than one man. She breathed slowly, concentrating on her breath, not the man, silently praying that he wouldn't decide to come closer. The other three were collecting their horses and mounting, calling him to follow. Finally, he stood, gave one last look up at the cave and turned to mount the horse that the others had brought to him. Even going through the pass, he had turned in the saddle for one last look.

Taking time to relax for a few moments, she turned her attention to her patient. He was conscious and watching her, breathing heavily. His right hand was clutching at his bound wound and she realised that he must be in pain.

"Have they gone?" he asked in Afrikaans as she walked over to him.

This was the first time he had said anything since this had all started. He had a soft voice for such a big man.

Lorraine nodded, "I want to make sure though. This evening, just before dark, I'll scout around to make sure they have left."

She knelt next to him to examine his wound, "We'll have to dig this bullet out before poisoning sets in, but not now. I want them to be far away when you start screaming like a baby."

She glanced up at his face. He had a slight smile.

"Sorry," she said, "that's from growing up with two brothers."

"Two," he said.

"Yes, two brothers, Willem and Walter," she replied.

"No, no, I meant two bullets."

Her blood ran cold. One was bad enough but two were going to be hell for him. They wouldn't be in the same hole, although the holes must be very close together.

"Ag well, one or two, makes no difference. I am not going to feel a thing," she tried to be light hearted.

He snorted but then gritted his teeth.

"I know what to expect," he finally said, "this isn't the first time."

"How do you feel right now?" she asked with concern, "do you think you could move out of here with my help?"

He half smiled again, "ja, just very hungry."

Lorraine smiled, "well you will just have to wait but I'll get more water."

She took her Mauser with her as she clambered down to the stream. It was the middle of the day now but although it was hot out in the sun, the cave was cool.

The eagle was a Martial Eagle and he watched all these proceedings with detached interest from four thousand feet. He had finished eating for the day and was now only interested in the cool currents. From his position up in the thermals, he could see into the *kloof* and the farmyard. The fire the day before had disturbed some Springhares and he had dined like the king of the air that he was.

He banked and watched the men ride away. He saw them stop as one took leave of his friends and turned south. The sun was low when the girl came cautiously through the pass. She skirted the farmyard until she felt safe and then headed back to the cave.

The sun was about to set when the girl emerged through the pass with the wounded man on the big black horse. He also saw, from his perch on the rock, how the man who had turned south, came walking his horse back toward the farmyard. His name was Skalk, not used to failure. He was wearing an old English bowler hat that he had mashed down in the middle of the crown. Even a way out from the farmyard, he heard the noise that the wounded man was making. He smiled; his hunch had paid off.

Lorraine knew that she had to remove the bullets while she still had good light. She quickly mixed some herbs together and added a good sprinkling of *dagga*. After she gave the mixture added to a bit of Buchu brandy to the man, she looked around. It was too dark in the barn so she walked him out to a table next to the hand-pump on the edge of the yard clearing.

Even with a chunk of wood in his mouth, he made a lot of noise while she dug the bullets out just below the shoulder. She bound the wound up with more honey-comb and then let him rest in his drugged sleep. The big black pricked up his ears and snorted.

Skalk waited at the edge of the clearing, looking around carefully. He had a good view of the barn but the burnt shell of the house blotted out the table where Lorraine was working on the man. His rifle lay across his saddle as he started working his way around the farmyard.

Lorraine had to chase a Martial Eagle away from the top of Leopard Rock before she could peer over into the farmyard. The man next to her grunted and she held a finger to her lips.

Darkness fell, his friends scattered
Hope seemed lost…
But heaven just started counting to three
From 'God's Not Lost'

CHAPTER 2

"What is your name?" she asked him softly, sliding down a few inches in the sand so that she was next to him.

"Gideon," he answered, "Gideon Barron."

"You can call me Rainkies," she said as she manoeuvred herself up to be able to look over the top of the rock.

There was a lot of bird droppings on top of the rock but she would have to put up with it. She couldn't risk raising dust for the man below to see. The eagle floated on the thermals, watching. He didn't mind the disturbance. He needed to hunt now anyway. This should be interesting but he dived sideways to scan a ploughed land a few miles away.

The top of the rock was about a hundred yards from the farmyard, as a bullet flies anyway. Lorraine held a small bush that she could see through, in front of her face. Gideon was trying to squirm into a comfortable position that wouldn't hurt his shoulder. He still felt light-headed from the herbs that he had drunk. He had recognised the taste of the Buchu brandy but not the faintly familiar after-taste of the herbs. They were up on the rock without any water or food. There hadn't been enough time to collect anything. It was by the width of a hair that they had managed to slip away.

Skalk was so frustrated he could spit bullets. He had been confident of catching them. He would summarily shoot the man but he had problems with the idea of shooting a woman. His upbringing wouldn't let him do it. The man was a traitor and deserved to die but now Skalk had lost them again. He had found the table covered with fresh blood and close by, the big black horse. The area around the table was too churned up to pick up any fresh spoor and, on top of that, it was starting to get dark fast. He took his horse and the big black into the barn and wiped them both down. There was water in a trough so he let them drink. At the very least, he was taking this horse with him. Of the horse that the fugitive had ridden in on, there was no sign.

There was biltong hanging in the rafters and Skalk found a table with dried peaches spread out on a large cotton cloth. He couldn't light a fire with those two out there. He would be a sitting duck to a Mauser bullet. There was some tobacco hanging in the rafters too so, settling down to a good pipe after his meagre supper, he lay down on an opened bale of feed and pulled his blanket close.

The Martial eagle brought a springhare back to his perch on the rock. The people had gone and he dismissed them from his mind.
Lorraine knew that Gideon's horse would look for water and Lorraine knew where the water was. She could find it with her eyes closed and so could also find it in the dark. It was a little way from the farmyard, a dam with a drinking trough and a windmill. They had to get as far away from the

farmyard as possible or kill this man following them. She couldn't kill unless he attacked them. She didn't know if Gideon would be able to and she was scared to ask.

Sure enough, the horse was there and seemed pleased to smell Gideon.

"Her name is Flam," said Gideon, "because of her reddish colour."

They walked a short distance north and then Lorraine insisted that Gideon climb up. She had to help him up.

"For a short while," she said, "and then I will ride up behind you."

After a short distance they found the path that Lorraine was looking for and she mounted behind him.

At one stage during the night, Gideon started falling forward and Lorraine had to pull him up. She called to him but he had lost consciousness. They were both very tired. The stress of the day had also taken its toll. When she saw that the moon was past its zenith, she pulled up and dismounted. There was a mound next to a tree that she remembered and pulled Gideon off toward her. He slid over, causing her to collapse to the ground. She lay panting for a few moments and then pushed him onto his good side before falling asleep herself.

Skalk was up at first light, searching for spoor. It didn't take him long to find their footprints leading away from the farmyard. They couldn't have gone far on foot, he reckoned. This time he was going to hunt slowly and methodically. The sun was pushing through the tree tops by the time he reached the top of Leopards Rock only to find scuff marks. A Martial Eagle dipped away onto the thermals as Skalk looked down onto the deserted farmyard.

He felt like throwing a tantrum but instead he searched the horizon in all directions to look for any movement or dust cloud. Very far to the north he saw a small dust cloud. It could be them or it could just be herd of buck on the move. It wouldn't hurt to take a look, he thought, as he slid down from the rock and ran back to where his horse still needed to be saddled up.

Gideon and Lorraine were letting Gideon's horse canter along the pathway.

"Where are we headed?" asked Gideon over his shoulder.

"My cousin has a farm to the east of Naboomspruit, on the far side of the Nyl river near to Immerpan," she answered.

"They will keep hunting me," said Gideon.

"Ja but I only want to hide you long enough so that you don't fall off your horse. Then you can go your own way and fight your own battles."

"You haven't asked why they are hunting me," said Gideon.

"Time enough for that. Then I might shoot you myself," answered Lorraine.

Gideon smiled and looked forward again. She might want to when she heard his story.

"I also have family up this way but I don't know exactly where," said Gideon.

He had heard spoken of family up this way but didn't even know their names. Lorraine didn't answer. She didn't know if her cousins would be on their farm. She had heard of the British taking the women and children into camps but hadn't heard anything from her family since her father and brothers had left to join the commando.

Gideon's shoulder was throbbing and blood was seeping from the bindings that the girl had used. They came down from the hills onto the Springbok Flats just before noon. Not long after that they crossed the northern railway line and headed into the swamplands of the Nyl. Gideon was holding the reins now.

"Try to keep out of the water," Lorraine warned him, "the leeches will get onto the horses' legs and our legs if we go deep enough. I haven't heard of crocodiles but you never know."

Gideon grunted, easier said than done. There were streams crossing their path that were impossible to miss. The air was muggy and hot in the swamp basin and Gideon's horse kept pulling toward the cooler water. There was no shade. The thorn trees were too low to stop under so they pushed forward to get to the far side. The swamp was only a few miles wide but the streams and pools slowed them down. When they reached the far side, Lorraine stepped down to check the horse, luckily no leeches.

Gideon was bleeding quite badly so she pulled him down and helped him to sit on a mound while she inspected his wound. It looked clean at least so she bound it up again. Maybe the bleeding cleaned it but he couldn't lose too much blood. She was sure he must've lost quite a bit all in all already.

They rested for a few minutes and drank water from one of the flowing streams before moving on. A storm was brewing over the Flats, dark clouds and lightning but still too far away to hear the thunder. During rainy season, this swamp became a wide, flowing river. Lorraine had spent holidays with her cousins here and had seen this beautiful swamp in flood. At it's peak, there was no way of getting across. It was said that when the *Voortrekkers*, the pioneers, reached here, the river was in flood and they thought that they had found the source of the Nile. Not a very believable story though because this river flowed south.

Lorraine recognised the area now and she led them north-east. They passed a number of small herds of Impala, fairly tame if you are on the back of a horse. The sun was behind them and a black sky in front of them, slowly sweeping toward them. When they rode into the farmyard, big individual drops were falling. The thunder was only minutes behind the lightning strikes now. A Syringa tree was in full bloom in the middle of the yard. A big yellow boerbull dog came off the veranda to meet them. He had given a bark as he came off the *stoep* but now as he recognised Lorraine, he wagged his tail and ran next to the horse.

Skalk sat his horse at the beginning of the swamp and watched the storm coming in. Even if he reached the far side, the rain would have washed the spoor away. For the second time in not long, he had to admit defeat. First the bitterness of hearing that a peace treaty was being signed, now knowing that the man who had played a part in that defeat, was going to get away from him. He turned his horse back toward the Naboomspruit hotel. At least he would sleep in a warm, soft bed with a full stomach.

The steam engine of the late afternoon train going north stood puffing in the station. He had to skirt behind the guard's van, around the green wood and iron buildings of the station before crossing the road and stopping at the hitch-rail in front of the hotel. He swung down and handed the reins to a young black boy to take care of his horse.

A light musty smell that he couldn't place, greeted him as he took his key and sought out his room facing the street. After taking a long bath in a soapy smelling bathroom, he went into the dining-room and took a table against the wall. It was his habit to sit with his back against the wall.

There were few people there but halfway through his meal he couldn't help noticing a group of four men at a table only a short distance from him. They had been drinking and didn't notice that they were talking loud enough for him to hear. They were bragging to each other about how they had become rich by taking gold from the Boers before the peace treaty had been signed. They were a section of a commando who unloaded the gold from a train coach in Pienaars River siding. They spoke about the place that they had hidden the gold and Skalk took careful note of it. They were dressed like Boers and were speaking Afrikaans. They must be Boers themselves thought Skalk. Then he heard something that rocked him.

They laughed as they told each other that all the blame would be placed on the head of a youngBoer by the name of Gideon Barron. They had come under attack while they were unloading the gold bullion onto wagons. They were ordered to move the wagons away from the fighting but had just kept going toward Mozambique. After a few days they had come to an agreement amongst themselves that they were going to hide the gold near Nelspruit.

Skalk waited for them to finish their meal and, with not much patience, for them to drink several cups of coffee. He thought to himself that he needed to let General Beyers know where the gold was. First, he was going to kill these traitors. They were each carrying a rifle but Skalk knew that he could shoot fast and straight with a Webley revolver that he had taken off a dead Englishman. He followed them out the front of the hotel, his Webley in his right hand hanging at his side.

Stepping down the step off the veranda, they turned when he called to them, his revolver already raised, pointing at the one he thought may be the best. Three went down before they realised what was happening, the fourth fired at the same time as Skalk. Skalk's bullet burst the arteries in the man's heart as the man pulled the trigger on his Mauser but the man's bullet found it's mark. Skalk wasn't going to be able to tell anybody anything.

His cheek was in the sand and he could see the bank across the street. A big drop of rain plopped into the dust in front of his eye but he didn't mind. Rain was good, they needed the rain. He felt the drops on his body but he seemed to be swimming, slowly away. It was getting dark fast and he thought he should be getting back to tell someone something, he couldn't remember what. Slowly he floated away to the sound of shouting in the distant.

Men ran from the hotel to the five men lying in the street. The storm was upon them and they lifted the men onto the veranda. A doctor among them felt for their pulses. One was still alive. The doctor shouted to the men around him. They lifted the wounded man and quickly carried him inside. A table was cleared by sweeping everything onto the floor. The man was trying to say something.

"Don't worry," said the doctor, "you are in good hands."

The doctor put his ear close to the man's lips to hear what he had to say.

"No," muttered the man, "it can't be, I am rich," but he had to learn that the rich as well as the poor must die in the end.

The doctor straightened up, "he is gone. He said he is rich. Does anyone here know him?"

Men crowded forward. They muttered amongst themselves but had to admit in the end, they had never seen him before today. Oh well, the newly formed Town Council would have to pay for the five funerals. Pity, they never had anything of value on them nor in their bags. The horses could be sold though.

"We don't know who they are so we can't even let their families know," said doctor Pieter Pretorious to his wife later that evening. "We don't even know where they come from."

"I suppose their families will think that they died in the war," said his wife, Anne.

Pieter grunted as he took another mouthful of his dinner. A shame, he thought. They must've known each other but why did they shoot each other? The storm raged outside, thunder and lightning. The paraffin lamp fluttered once when lightning struck particularly close.

"The Nyl will flood I suppose," Pieter said around mouthful of meat, "I won't be able to get to anyone out on the Flats if they need me."

"Pieter, don't speak with your mouth full," his wife scolded him.

Pieter grunted again, not taking much notice of her.

The storm had petered out across the Flats now. A rainbow appeared in the east for a short period. The Nyl was indeed rising and would soon be in flood as night came. The leaves on the trees were dripping. The farmyard near Immerpan was muddy. Luckily the horses had already been put in the barn as the storm had started. They were warm, fed and dried.

"We don't have much chance of getting a doctor out here, Rainkies," Lorraine's cousin, Zandra, told her. "The Nyl is sure to flood after that storm."

Lorraine's forehead was lined with worry. "We will have to doctor him ourselves."

Gideon smiled to himself, he had never had two good looking girls looking after him before. He did feel weak, more than likely from the loss of blood. Zandra put a basin of warm water on the kitchen table and Lorraine carefully took the dressing off his wound.

"Well?" He asked humorously, "do you think I'll live?"

"Not funny," Lorraine glared at him.

He kept quiet after that. Zandra put a few drops from a bottle into the basin of water. Lorraine dabbed at the wound with a clean cloth.

"*Eina,*" Gideon jumped.

Whatever it was in the water stung the open flesh.

"Keep still," Lorraine admonished him, "not so tough, *ne.*"

She cleaned the wound and then bound it up again with clean bandages that Zandra brought out.

The thunder had also died away to the west. The back door was open so they heard the frogs in full croak. Geel, the dog was sitting at the door watching the girls work on the man. It was dark outside, Gideon smiled at the dog and nodded. Geel seemed to acknowledge the nod with two swishes of his tail. Maybe he sensed that this man was hurt and needed help. The dog heard a noise at the edge of the bush and half turned his head before realising that it was just a harmless animal. He turned back to study the man.

Zandra had a stew going on the wood stove. The smell was making Gideon's stomach clench. Geel knew that, if he was patient, he would get a bowl full. Zandra brought a clean shirt to Gideon.

"My father's," she said.

"Are you sure it will be alright?" Gideon asked as he took it thankfully.

"My father won't mind me helping another human being," she answered.

She fashioned a sling from a large white cloth and the two girls helped him hold up his arm and tie it over his shoulder. He was aware of their smell when they were so close. His bible was in his bag and he would need to put it under his pillow tonight or he would never get to sleep. Even the pain in his shoulder didn't stop his mind run away with him

The girls cleared the table and set a white table-cloth with knives and forks. The stew of chopped beef and vegetables tasted delicious. He had a second helping and was thinking of a third when he looked up and saw the dog watching him so he settled for a slice of milk tart and coffee. As he sat back with a second cup, he noticed that the girls were watching him.

"Has he explained yet how he came to be wounded?" Zandra asked Lorraine.

"No," Lorraine answered, "I have been waiting for him to be fully conscious."

Gideon noticed then that Zandra had a rifle across her lap.

"Hopefully it's a good story," she was serious, "we may have to shoot him again."

"Boers were chasing him," said Lorraine.

"Why did you save him then?" asked Zandra.

"No idea," Lorraine answered, "maybe only the fact that they looked as if they meant to kill him. We could hand him in at the local commando."

"The commando isn't back from the war yet. We can't hold him so we may have to kill him," Zandra looked tense.

Gideon hoped they were joking but it didn't look like it. "I will tell you what happened."

If you tell the truth
You don't have to remember anyth
Mark Twain

CHAPTER 3

This was Gideon's story. He told the truth with all
sincerity hoping they would believe him.

"We had hoped to have another go at the Brits when
our commando was sent north from Witbank. Talking
amongst ourselves we speculated about which
regiment we would be dealing with. The Gordon
Highlanders had a reputation of being fierce fighters
and excitement ran high with the thought of meeting
them in battle.

We were supposed to leave at first light but the sun
was drawing water by the time we rode out. Our front
riders chased an elephant out of our way as we went
through the *kloof*, eighty riders, eager to taste battle. It
was obvious, to me anyway, that the Brits were
winning this war. Our hero, De la Rey, had smashed
the English at Tweebosch in March but since then we

had one defeat after the other. Kitchener was pouring British soldiers into the Transvaal. The British newspapers were saying that there were three hundred and sixty thousand British troops in South Africa now and we were running out of ammunition. The rumour was that Holland and Germany were sending us arms and ammunition but we hadn't seen anything of them yet.

Anyway, my thoughts were more on fighting the English. Coming from an Irish background we naturally fought with the side against the English. I didn't hate them as some of the Boers did but my loyalty lay completely with the Boer cause. All my close friends were Boers and now I rode with two of them, men who I had grown up with, Tinus and Jaco. I also spoke Afrikaans like a Dutchman.

When we reached the Pienaars River, there was a Veldkornet with a few men waiting for us. Our Commandant spoke to the Veldkornet and then rode back to where we had dismounted and spoke to us. We were taking the opportunity to water the horses.

"Veldkornet Viljoen needs six volunteers to ride with him," he said, dismounting beside us.

"To do what?" asked Jaco.

Jaco never did like changing plans. Anyway, my dad always taught us never to volunteer for anything so I kept my head down.

"To pick up ammunition and take it to the commandoes fighting in the Drakensburg near Nelspruit," our Commandant answered.

Well that didn't sound like fun. We all wanted to go to where the fiercest battle was raging. Nobody said a word.

"Well if nobody wants to volunteer, I will have to choose the men, Van Deventer," he looked at Jaco, "you can be one."

As soon as Jaco was called, Tinus stuck up his hand, "I will go Commandant," he called.

So I had to stick up my hand, "I'll go."

Reluctantly three others put up their hands.

We mounted as soon as our horses were ready and rode over to Viljoen's group. There were ten of us altogether including the Veldkornet. We followed the river west.

I rode up beside one of the original group, "do you know where we are going?" I asked.

He grunted and looked at me as if I was a worm that had just crawled out from under a rock, "of course I know," he snarled at me.

I was a bit taken back.

"I don't know why we needed you back riders," he carried on.

Well that was a derogatory remark and my hair stood up on the back of my neck. I was about to urge my horse into his when Viljoen chipped in, telling us to keep quiet.

"We are passing a possible British camp," he said, only loud enough for us to hear.

My face was burning as I fell back to join Tinus and Jaco.

"Don't worry," Jaco said with a smile on his face, "I'll shoot him in the back, if we ever get a chance to go into battle again."

I wasn't sure if he was joking but it made me smile too.

I thought I should keep an eye on that man. I didn't even know his name.

We walked our horses until we were clear of the possible British camp and then Viljoen ordered us into a canter. Tinus had spoken to one of the other men, a Clarence Meintjies, who told him that we were headed to the Pienaars River siding on the Northern rail-line. Apparently, this Clarence wasn't at all friendly either. I couldn't understand it. Why didn't they want our help? Tinus just shrugged it off but it worried me. Things were getting serious for us Boers and I thought the hard times would pull us closer together.

We had all seen friends and family fall to British guns. Luckily none of my family that I knew of but I had watched some good friends go down in the heat of battle. Something that scars your attitude for life, I would think.

While we rode, I let my mind wonder on what I was going to do at the end of this war. I would carry on fighting to the end but I could already see the writing on the wall. If I could go on what we had heard, it was said, with some pride, that the Boers had thirty-nine thousand fighting men in the field. I knew from experience that a lot of them were *penkoppe*, young boys under the age of sixteen. We knew that we were losing more battles than we were winning. It was only pride that kept us going. We were outnumbered almost ten to one but we kept fighting. We couldn't imagine a country under British rule again.

As I said, I didn't hate the British as much as some but I would need to do something, after the war, where I wouldn't come in contact with them on a daily basis. I didn't have a farm and my Dad would still work his for many years and his farm couldn't keep two families. As far as I knew, he was still alive and I prayed that he would stay alive for many more years.

I was still deep in thought when the riders in front of me started pulling up.

"We are getting close, men," said Viljoen, "and I don't know what the situation is here right now."

He called two of his original men forward and sent them ahead to spy out the lay of the land. They walked their horses ahead as we dismounted and waited for them. It didn't take them long. They were soon back. They stopped a little way in front of us and motioned us to come on. When we reached them, they spoke to Viljoen.

"The train is there, waiting for us," I heard one say to Viljoen, "the doors are open and the wagons are standing ready."

Viljoen motioned us forward and we moved through the bush out to the clearing on either side of the track and siding. The siding was obviously for loading farm produce and cattle. Right now, it was being used to load ammunition boxes from a train truck onto three ox-wagons.

"Come men," Viljoen called, "we need to move this load before the *Khakies* upset things."

We dismounted at a hitchrail near a green, wood and iron building.

"Things don't look right," said Tinus.

Jaco and I turned to study the scene.

"What you mean?" Jaco asked as we walked toward the truck.

"Those boxes look very heavy," answered Tinus.

"Well they are full of ammo," said Jaco.

I never said anything, Tinus maybe right.

The rail-line was raised above the ground on fist sized rocks that appeared to have come from the gold mines. The boxes were slid down by men unloading from the truck. We helped those catching the boxes at the bottom and loading them onto the wagons. There was a short platform but it would be too short for a wagon with a full span of oxen.

Tinus was right, the boxes were ammunition boxes but two men struggled to handle one box.

"What do you think is in them?" I asked Tinus as we walked back after loading our first box.

"Only gold and lead are that heavy," answered Tinus, "and I doubt it's lead."

I peeled off to where Viljoen was still on his horse, shouting orders.

"Veldkornet, what is all this about?" I asked him.

He swung down and stood face to face with me.

"This is Republic gold," he said quietly, "we managed to smuggle it out of the mines in Jo'burg after the British moved in. It must be taken to the port in Lorenco Marques to pay for the arms and ammunition coming from our supporters."

"Why didn't they just put it on the Mozambique line?" I asked.

He grunted. "They didn't have a choice. The British nearly caught them and stopped the train but they managed to get away. You can be sure that the British are not far behind."

He stepped away from me and started shouting orders again.

I stumbled back to where Tinus was waiting for me and explained quickly as we struggled with the next box. As soon as one wagon was full, they pulled it away and drove the next one into place. The full wagons kept going, moving east toward the coast. I had always thought that my hands were tough from hard work but I suppose they had softened these two years at war. They were red and saw by the time the

second wagon was loaded and on its way. We loaded
into the evening

We took it in turns to stop for a drink of water and
take a few minutes rest but we all felt the urgency and
so didn't stop for long. We were almost finished
loading the third wagon when a cry was heard from
down the line to the south. This was followed by a
shot.

"Faster men!" Viljoen cried out and the Commandant
mounted and rode after the first of the wagons. "there
is a loco coming up the track!"

We managed to finish loading but could see the
lightbeam from the front of the locomotive coming at
full steam up the line through the bush. The land was
very flat in this area, just before Warmbad so we
could see some distance.

The call came to mount and we all ran for our horses
but by the time we were crossing the tracks, the Loco
was almost upon us. Shots rang out from the
oncoming train and we could here bullets pinging off
the empty truck still on the track.

"My men will escort the wagons!" shouted Viljoen and we followed him at a gallop.

I glanced over my shoulder to see the other men spreading out in a skirmish line, I supposed to delay anyone trying to follow us. Some men were heading to hide behind the empty truck, others were making for the bush line.

I saw Viljoen go down and I swung down while my horse was still on the move. I slapped his rump to keep him moving and out the way. A few running steps took me to where Viljoen was lying. He was on his back and fading fast.

"Bastards," he murmured before blood oozed through his lips.

"What?" I asked but he stared at me and I watched as the life faded from his eyes.

I looked toward the wagons but they were disappearing into the dark bush. Turning back toward the train, a battle was raging. Then I noticed that Viljoen had been shot in the chest. This could only mean that someone, one of his own men, had shot him.

I started walking toward the train when I felt a punch in my shoulder. I went down onto my knees. I struggled to stay upright, not feeling any pain, but saw the ground coming up to meet me. I could feel damp leaves against my cheek. Why damp, I wondered. I heard shouting as night slowly closed in.

When I came around, I was sitting on a chair. Pain suddenly shot through my shoulder and I saw that a man, who I didn't recognise, was squeezing my shoulder.

"What happened to the wagons?" he shouted at me. I tried to clear my head. I didn't know what he meant. Slowly the realization dawned on me, the wagons with the gold must've disappeared. Then he was squeezing my shoulder again.

"I don't know, I don't know," I tried to squirm away from his hand but he held on.

"They rode away from me," I said, wincing. "I saw Viljoen go down and stopped to help him."

"So why is he dead," the man shouted.

I don't know why he was shouting; I was right there but I suppose it was the adrenaline that was making him shout.

"He was already dead," I said. No use telling this madman that he was still alive.

The man half turned and I saw that other men, obviously Boers, were standing around. I noticed that we were in a train truck. The man that had been questioning me was sobbing.

Another man took over, "how did they get away so quickly?" he asked, still shouting but not as high pitched as the other man.

"I don't know!" I was raising my voice now and got smacked in the mouth for it.

"Let me shoot him, Veldkornet," said a mean looking man standing to one side.

"Don't be stupid," said the one who had hit me, obviously the Veldkornet, "we have to make him tell us where the gold is."

He turned back to me, "do you realize that the gold was our only chance to buy badly needed arms and ammunition."

"I didn't know there was gold in the boxes," I answered.

"Stupid!" he screamed and hit me in the mouth again, "what did you think is in the boxes, feathers," and hit me again just for good measure.

I hadn't taken a beating as bad as this since I started school and the older boys found out that I wasn't Afrikaans, or Dutch back then.

Just then a man stuck his head through the sliding door of the truck, "Veldkornet, there is another train coming."

Everyone started scrambling for the door.

"What should we do with him?" asked the man who had been sobbing.

"Leave him," answered the Veldkornet, "we can come back for him. If the *Khakis* kill him, too bad."

It was quiet in the coach for a few minutes but then I heard the other loco, chugging at full speed, getting closer. I struggled with the thongs binding my hands behind the chair and my ankles lashed to the chair legs. All I managed to do was turn the chair over. I wasn't sure what would be the worse fate, to be taken prisoner by the British or to be taken by the Boers again. I decided to face the Boers. Surely they would listen to reason eventually.

There were bales of feed in the one end of the truck and I scraped my way, still tied to the chair, in that direction. I hadn't reached them yet when I heard the loco screeching with its brakes full on. My chair scraping on the floor sounded very loud to me but I knew that there was so much noise outside, they wouldn't hear me. I managed to get a bale to fall half across between me and the door. Outside it was chaos. The other train must've collided with the trucks that I was on. There was a tremendous crash, I slid in a full circle and bales of feed flew all over the place. I was well screened from the door now.

There was a thunder of gun shots with men shouting. It seemed to carry on for ages. It was dark in the truck now and eventually the sound of shots became less and men slowly stopped shouting. I heard English commands but that didn't help me at all. Dressed the way I was and with the adrenaline still pumping through their veins, they would shoot me on sight. I heard English shouts at the door of my truck and I stayed quiet. One man seemed to climb into the doorway but then jump off again, shouting as he did. Although I knew he was shouting in English, I couldn't understand what he was saying. He had a heavy accent, maybe from northern England. After some time, the noise died down and the loco puffed as it moved away, I suppose backward, the way it had come.

With my chair being thrown around in the crash, the thongs holding me had loosened slightly. I frantically worked on them and first managed to get my hands out. After that it didn't take long before I was completely free. My shoulder was aching. Maybe aching was the wrong word. Pain had taken over the whole of my upper body but I knew that, if I wanted to stay alive, I needed to get out of there fast.

Luckily the truck had moved in line with the siding platform so that the floor of the truck was level with the platform. I didn't think I would've been able to jump down. Morning was close. I like to think that I ran toward the place where I thought my horse must be. In truth, I must've stumbled along. My horse was in the bush near to where I had left him. Getting on was a different story. My arms were almost useless but half throwing, half pulling, I managed to mount. I pulled him around toward the Waterburg mountains and heeled him into a gallop. On my way over the tracks, I heard a shout. This time it was the unmistakeable sound of the Afrikaans tongue. I urged my horse faster and I could hear the thunder of horse's hooves behind me. Shots rang out as I weaved through the bush. I thought that I had managed to get away and turned in my saddle. I saw a flash and I felt the now familiar punch in the shoulder. The pain didn't change but I was worried about blood loss.

I fell in and out of consciousness but managed to stay heads up and in front. I could feel the foothills under my horses' hooves but kept going. My followers must've fallen slightly behind but there was no doubt that they would hunt me down like a mad dog that they thought I was. When I came around, I thought that I had made it to heaven. I smelt clean soap and an angel was helping me off my horse."

Ad hominem

Latin Quotation

To the person (to appeal to feelings rather than reason)

CHAPTER 4

Gideon slumped back in the chair. The room was quiet as he finished his story. The girls were both looking at him.

All of a sudden Zandra stood up, "do we believe him?" she asked no one in particular.

Lorraine looked up at her, waiting for her to speak again. Zandra still held her rifle.

"Rainkies, why should we believe him?"

Gideon felt her stare. He knew she wasn't convinced. If he was facing two men, his reaction may have been different but these two young women had first shown compassion before questioning him. He wouldn't be able to hurt them anyway.

Zandra sighed and turned away toward the stove and busied herself with something, banging pots and pans.

"I don't know what to do to prove this to you," said Gideon to Lorraine.

"We will think about it," Lorraine answered, "in the meantime if you make a wrong move, we will kill you."

"After you saved me?" Gideon asked with a half-smile.

"Maybe that was a mistake," answered Lorraine. She wasn't smiling.

She watched him carefully and Gideon struggled to relax under her gaze. After the meal and coffee, he knew that he was going to need the toilet. When he asked, Lorraine motioned him up with her rifle. It was about twenty yards from the house. Lorraine sat on the back veranda with him in her sights. He wouldn't have run anyway. Where could he go? Lorraine looked more at ease when he again walked back toward her. She followed him into the kitchen. Zandra was sitting at the table and they joined her.

"I think we are going to have to go back to Pienaars River," said Zandra.

Gideon was quiet. He didn't think that was a good idea.

"What are we going to find there?" asked Lorraine, "are we going to hand him over?"

Gideon tensed up.

"Maybe, maybe not," answered Zandra, "depends on what we find there."

"What are you hoping to find?" asked Gideon. Zandra's look was not very friendly, "anything that will show that you are telling the truth." She looked at Lorraine, "if he is telling the truth, he will need us to help him clear himself. If he is lying, we need to hand him over, dead or alive."

Her determination made Gideon smile inside but he kept his face serious. He somehow hoped that they would come to believe him. He owed them his life but the minute he felt that his life was in danger again, he would make a break for it.

"First he must get his strength back and his wound must heal," said Zandra, "he is not much use to us the way he is now."

Well, thought Gideon, he could agree with that. The food was good anyway. He got up and walked out onto the back veranda. They didn't move to stop him. Geel joined him and lay at his feet. At least someone was friendly. He sat there for a long time, the sun set and the guinea-fowl were chirring out in the bush, looking for a perch out of reach of jackals. He relaxed and tried to imagine his wounds healing. There was a steady throb in his chest. He knew from experience that it would take at least a week before he could sit a horse comfortably. It wouldn't be healed but at least it wouldn't bleed, if he took it easy. He wondered if the girls had experience of someone healing from a gunshot wound. They seemed to be strong-willed and intelligent enough.

The smell of cooking drifted out the back door and Gideon felt at ease as he slapped at a mosquito on his neck sending a sharp pain through his chest. In spite of the pain, he smiled. Two women nursing him, for a while, what more could a man ask for. He was still smiling when they ordered him in to come in and eat.

It took what seemed like forever before the girls would let him swing an axe but, in the meantime, he walked around as much as possible. They didn't mind him walking around in the bush but got all jumpy if he went near the horses. They didn't want him riding off. He loved the bush so walked quietly around watching animals. He prided himself at being able to get very close to *duiker* and *steenbokke*, two very shy buck. He wished he could shoot for the pot but couldn't risk opening the wound with the kick of the rifle. Geel kept him company. The yellow dog seemed to know when to lay still or stop in mid step when an animal was sighted.

The days passed and he slowly regained his strength. The day came when he could swing up into the saddle. That night they sat around the kitchen table with the paraffin lamp in the middle, planning. They had no news of the progress of the war but assumed that it must be over. Zandra's father and brothers hadn't come home so she was eager to get to a place where she could get some news of the men. They decided to ride straight south until they reached the

Pienaars river. If they kept the Waterburg mountains on the right, they were sure to reach the river as it curved to the west.

All three of them carried Mausers and Zandra had a store of 9mm ammunition under the floorboards. Meat was pre-cooked, eggs were packed carefully and of course they didn't forget the coffee. The coffee was cleared out, they took the last of it.
Gideon didn't really want to leave, thinking there wasn't much future in trying to prove his story and prove his innocence. He didn't think anyone was going to believe him unless they actually found the gold. Gideon lay on his bed that night with his head full of thoughts. These girls were putting themselves in danger for his sake. In particular he had an ache when around Lorraine. He supposed it was because she had saved him from certain death. He also wondered about Zandra's father and brothers. They could be dead or they could be part of these bitter-enders, the so called *bittereinders*. This lot had sworn to fight to the death.

They left at daybreak, Geel trotting beside Gideon's horse. The sun came up on their left over the Flats, to a day that promised to become stinking hot. The girls wanted to stop off that evening at a friend's farm so they followed a wagon track leading south that would take them near. Three black women carrying bundles of saplings on their heads, most probably for hut building, moved off the track for the horses to pass. Zandra spoke to them in North Sotho. They told her that all the farms in the district were deserted. The men hadn't come back from the war and the women and children were either in the big towns or in the British concentration camps.

The sun was still three fingers above the horizon when they came over the rise leading down to the friend's farm. They were just in time to hear two shots. Anyone who has heard rifle shots never forgets the sound. It is like a clap with a short echo. The girls sat straight up in the saddle.

"Something is very wrong," said Zandra.

They broke into a canter until they were about a hundred yards from the farmyard and then split up to come in from different sides. Gideon slid off his horse as he reached the edge of the clearing. There was nobody in sight. He heard shouting coming from the house and then someone shouted from the bush close to where he was crouched. He only caught an occasional word but both people were shouting in Afrikaans. He crept closer and saw a man, obviously a Boer, standing behind a *kameeldoring* tree.

"How could you do this?" he shouted. There was anger but the shout was almost a sob.

Zandra and Lorraine had reached the back yard and were crouching as they ran toward the back door of the farmhouse. Gideon slowly crept toward the man in the bush. He looked younger than Gideon. His clothes hung on his body, almost rags. If they were his clothes, he must've lost a lot of weight. His horse was a little way behind him and he was concentrating so hard on the house that he didn't hear Gideon nearing him.

"Who is that with you," he shouted, his voice changing, sharper.

He brought his rifle up to his shoulder. By this time Gideon was only about ten feet away from him to the side.

"Don't do it!" shouted Gideon.

The man started turning, by this time Gideon was five feet from him. Gideon's punch connected just in front of the man's ear. He went down like a sack of potatoes. By the time he reached the farmhouse with the man across his back, the girls were out on the front veranda. They had another woman, about their age, and a man with them. Gideon dumped the man on the floor as two kids came out the front door, a girl and a boy. The girl looked about ten years old and the boy a little younger. They grabbed hold of the woman; the young girl was whimpering. Their clothes looked old but clean.

"Gideon, this is Soekie," said Lorraine, pointing to the woman, "and these are her children, Suzan and Dirk, and this," she said with a bit of contempt in her voice, turning to the man, "is mister Johan Spies." Gideon grunted, "so what's the story here?"

"Well we were just waiting to hear the story ourselves," Lorraine answered and turned to Soekie.

"We thought Jan was dead," Soekie burst out, "a rider from his commando brought the news a year ago already."

Johan was nodding furiously.

"And now Jan just walked into the house this afternoon. We were in the kitchen; I was getting ready to make supper. He took one look at Johan and went beserk. I tried to talk to him," said Soekie with despair in her voice, "but he was screaming and shouting."

Johan was still nodding furiously.

"He threatened to shoot us all, including the children so when he lifted his Mauser, Johan shot into the floor in front of him. He ran out the front door and has been shouting at us from the bush. He wouldn't listen to me."

"So now we are listening," Zandra said sternly.

Johan moved to the side.

"No, no," Lorraine warned him but he was only going to sit on a chair.

Zandra motioned Soekie to carry on.

"Johan has been visiting and helping us for some months now since he got back from commando," Soekie had desperation in her voice again. "I was trying to explain to Jan. We thought Jan was dead."

Jan was stirring. Gideon bent to help him. When Jan saw where he was, he started scrambling up with a roar so Gideon hit him again.

"I don't think we can stay the night here," said Gideon, to no one in particular.

"You have to help me explain to Jan," Soekie was starting to wail again.

Gideon looked at Lorraine, "I've got nothing," he said, "Never been in this situation before."

It was quiet in the room for a few minutes. The two children stood quiet. The girl was hanging onto her mother. The boy was standing, trying to look defiant but looked very forlorn.

"What I suggest is that Zandra and I ride on but Johan better come with us," said Lorraine. "Jan will kill Johan if he sees him, he is not going to listen to reason."

"Gideon, will you stay and wait until Jan calms down?"

"I don't know what to say to him," Gideon protested.

"I will do the talking," said Soekie, "you must just make sure he doesn't kill us."

Gideon wasn't happy, "I would rather face my enemies," he said, "anyway, I thought you wanted to keep an eye on me."

"Pft," Lorraine blew through her lips as she turned away.

"I don't even know where you are going," said Johan, looking around the room.

"Do you want to be hunted down?" asked Zandra.

"Please go with them," pleaded Soekie, looking at Johan.

"How will I find you?" asked Gideon.

"We are going to another friend, further south. Her name is Hester. Ask Soekie later, she will direct you," answered Zandra.

They watched Johan mount up with the two girls and ride south, the setting sun on their right.

"They won't make it before dark," remarked Soekie with concern.

"And Johan doesn't even have a blanket," said Gideon.

"Oh he does," said Soekie with wide eyes, "he wasn't going to sleep here. He was going back to his own farm further north."

Now he was moving south. It wasn't that Johan was scared of Jan but for Soekie's sake he wanted to avoid any unpleasantness. He had to admit he had been aiming to court Soekie. That was before Jan came back. He had always loved Soekie but now, looking back, maybe it was more of a brotherly love. He knew where they were going. He had been friends with Hester and her husband Piet since school days. They had always come together when their parents held dances in their barns. The boys came to look at the girls and the girls came to look at the boys while their parents danced. These things usually ended up in the boys fighting in a big free-for-all with the girls cheering them on, good fun. They parents could never figure-out where all the peach-brandy disappeared to.

When it became too dark to see, they stopped and made camp. Johan made the fire; the girls prepared a good supper. There were still lions around this part of the world so they had to keep the fire going all night. The only animal that would come near a fire was a rhino but there hadn't been rhinos here for a long time, not since Johan could remember anyway. Jackals were calling in the distance and the crickets were singing as Johan fell asleep.

When Lorraine kicked him awake it was still dark. "Your turn," she said and turned away.

The sun was pushing its head above the east when Johan kicked sand on the still smouldering embers and they swung into the saddle.

Gideon had spent an eventful night, keeping Jan subdued. He had tried talking to him but in the end had to hit him again. After that Soekie helped him tie Jan's ankles and wrists with leather *riempies*. When he came around again, they let him struggle until he started getting tired when Soekie started speaking to him. Eventually he stopped to listen, shouting in frustration which later turned to tears. At that point Soekie had him in her arms and they were sobbing together.

Gideon managed to get in some sleep before dawn. He easily picked up the spoor of the others moving in the direction that Soekie had given him, the yellow dog running beside him. The sun was directly above him, or close, when he reached the canyon that should be halfway to Hester and Piet's farm. Apart having to skirt a lion kill, he made good time. Even so, the sun was reaching for the Waterberg mountains in the west by the time he rode down a slope toward the smoke coming from the chimney of a farm house on the edge of a half-ploughed field.

The girls came out onto the front veranda to meet him and Geel went a bit crazy with excitement when he saw the girls. Johan came out and took his reins as he swung down. Lorraine took his hand shyly and gave it a squeeze. Nobody smiled and Gideon sensed that something was wrong.
"Where are your friends?" he asked.

Zandra nodded toward the front door.

"Hester is not well," said Zandra, "Piet brought her back from the British detention camp a few days back. She is just skin and bone."

"Weren't they given food?" Gideon asked.

"Piet says that the big problem was that the Boer women refused to eat in protest. They wouldn't take British medicine either. He says many women and children had died.

They separated the orphans from the other women, I suppose to persuade them to eat."

"Hester is very weak but I can't find anything else wrong with her, just malnutrition," said Lorraine.

"Well Lorraine is a good doctor," answered Zandra.

"I know," said Gideon, "she saved me."

Lorraine gave his hand another squeeze.

They walked inside. Piet stood up from where he had been stooping beside an armchair. He was a big man, easily as big as Gideon but a bit on the skinny side, more than likely because he hadn't been eating well during the last weeks of fighting. He shook Gideon's hand.

"Welcome to my house," he said, "this is my wife, Hester. Sorry, my wife isn't able to cook for us."

A red-haired woman lay back in the armchair, "Welcome."

Her face was drawn and her clothes hung on her.

Zandra clicked her tongue, "You men move outside, we will take over here."

Gideon moved onto the veranda with Piet and Johan. They pulled chairs up to a table.

"We were told to fetch our wives from the detention centre near Cullinan when we were handing our rifles over to the British. It was terrible. There were only a few Boer men there, mainly women with children. Very basic accommodation but the women kept it clean at least. Hester told me that they tried a hunger strike but the British took no notice."

"And did you hand in your rifle?" asked Johan.

"Ha," snorted Piet, "my old Martini yes."

Zandra came out with a tray of coffee cups and a plate of rusks.

"Lorraine is feeding Hester with some chicken soup," she said.

"I have been trying to look after her," said Piet with a tired voice.

"Lorraine says Hester will get better but it will take time. You will have to have patience," added Zandra.

"Do you have any help?" asked Johan, pointing toward the half-ploughed land.

"Yes," answered Piet, "the farm workers started arriving back yesterday.

Mosquitoes were starting to bite when they moved inside. The girls had mixed up a good supper of meat, potatoes and pumpkin and, of course, coffee. It was comfortable sitting around the table sipping coffee in the light of a fancy paraffin lamp. Gideon and Johan shared a room with two comfortable beds.

"I could get use to this," Gideon said softly to himself.

Gideon woke to a cock crowing under his window. He swung his legs to the floor and had a look between the curtains, it was starting to get light. The girls insisted on making breakfast first, mainly for Hester and Piet's benefit, so the sun was about to break out over the trees in the east when they finally swung up into the saddle.

The track they were following was narrow so they rode single file, Gideon in front and Johan at the back. The bush thinned out when they passed close to the base of Kranskop mountain.

There is a legend that, many years ago, a local chief tested the loyalty of his subjects by making them jump off the cliffs to their death. They passed a few herds of Impala with a number of Wildebeest among them.

Johan rode up beside Gideon. "You haven't told me where we are going yet," he said to Gideon.

"Ag yes, slipped my mind," answered Gideon, "I am not too sure myself but we are headed for Pienaars River siding to start with, after that your guess is as good as mine."

"But why?" asked Johan.

"Well we will be looking for gold." Gideon had a half smile on his face.

It was serious though. That was the only way he was going to prove his innocence. They had to at least find out what happened to the gold. The best place to start was at the siding where he had last seen the wagons disappearing east. They were close to the railroad now and followed a course parallel to it moving south.

> **At night when finally alone,**
> **I close my eyes-and I am home.**
> **I kneel and touch the blood-warm sand**
> **And feel the pulse beneath my hand**
> *Michelle Yd Frost*

CHAPTER 5

They sat their horses on the edge of the clearing to the siding. No activity except for a mangy looking dog laying on the platform. Geel growled low in his throat.

"Quiet Geel," commanded Zandra softly.

He relaxed, as if to say, 'well you handle it then.'

A man came out of the green, wood and iron building on the platform and started walking down to the southern end of the raised platform. The dog got up and followed him. It was midday and shimmering hot. The man looked uncomfortable in his pin-striped trousers, white shirt and black cap. Far to the south a plume of black smoke was spreading in the clear blue sky.

"Train coming," said Johan unnecessarily.

They sat in silence for a few more minutes.

"We don't have to go near the siding," said Gideon, "this is the side we were on with the wagons. The track they followed must be level with the siding, moving east."

"Well, you lead the way," said Lorraine looking at Gideon.

The land was flat again, the southern end of the Springbok Flats, part of the inland sea that had dried up thousands of years ago. Sea shells had been found around here. It was hot and dusty with some greenery alongside the river.

"We should water the horses," said Gideon, "the track moves east and the river moves south east so we don't know when we will see water again."

They all nodded agreement so they moved down into the shade of the willow trees that someone had planted there and swung down. The surrounding thorn trees didn't give much shade and you never knew what else was looking for shade there. At this time of day every living creature was trying to get out of the sun. The water was cool and flowing. They steered clear of the stagnant pools where Bilharzia was likely to breed.

They walked to the track once the horses had drunk their fill. There wouldn't be any spoor to follow but it was a good guess the wagons would've followed it. The going would have been too tough through the bush.

"This is like searching with a blind guide," said Zandra in disgust, "we don't have any idea what they had in mind or where they planned to go."

"I think if they turned off the track, with those heavy wagons, they would've left some sort of mark, broken branches or moved boulders," answered Gideon.

They spread out with two riding on each side of the track, Johan and Zandra on the left and Lorraine and Gideon on the right. They had only ridden about an hour when they saw a thin trail of smoke reaching above the trees ahead and the sound of children playing. It turned out to be a black family. The man and woman were sitting next to a fire and two young boys playing in the water of a stream. The woman wore a dress of grey to green colour. The man was dressed in Boer clothing but both of them barefoot. Clothing was laid out on the grass nearby, maybe just been washed in the river. Geel growled again, Zandra quietened him again.

"*Sabona,*" Zandra greeted them in South Sotho, "are you well?"

The man stood up as a sign of respect when addressing a woman, eyeing the dog. "*Yebo,*" he answered, "are you well?"

The woman kept quiet, leaving the talking to her husband. Gideon dismounted and stood in front of the man.

"Do you live nearby," Gideon asked the man.

"*Yebo,*" he answered, "this way," he indicated with his hand, his arm outstretched, "but I have only returned from the war, yesterday."

"And you?" asked Gideon, nodding to the woman, "have you been away?"

The woman started scrambling to her feet.

"Please sit," said Gideon.

She sank back to the grass, "no, I have been here."

"Did you see heavy wagons go in this direction some time ago?" he asked her.

"Yes, some time ago."

"How many?" he asked.

She held up four fingers and pointed along the track they were following.

"Stay well," they all echoed.

"Go well," the couple said together.

There was a stony crossing about a foot deep. The water was clear and they allowed their horses to take a few mouthfuls on the way through. Geel crouched in the water, tongue hanging out, cooling himself down. They kept riding with the sun reaching for the mountains behind them, looking for any indication that the wagons had left the track. They made good time but by nightfall they had found nothing. They rode until it was impossible to pick up any spoor and then let their horses find a way into a *donga* where the water from many rains had eroded a canyon into the floor of the Flats.

Grilling a piece of meat over the coals of their fire felt homely but Gideon knew that his reputation and perhaps his life depended on them finding evidence of his story. Lorraine may have some feeling for him but he had no doubt that Zandra wouldn't hesitate before putting another bullet in him. If it came to that, he would have to make a break for it. He didn't see himself shooting any of this group. As if reading his mind, Zandra challenged him.

"So, Gideon Barron, what do you think happened to the wagons?"

"Well, what we were supposed to do was take these wagons to Delegoa Bay to pay for arms and ammunition. Obviously, they deviated from the route, why otherwise would those men try to kill me as a traitor," it was a statement, not a question.

Everyone was quiet for a while.

"It must have happened soon after your skirmish with the British," said Johan. Zandra had told him the story while they had been riding.

"That's true," Gideon agreed, "it must've happened, at the most, within the first hour of their travel."

"That means we have come too far from the siding. We need to go back and retrace our steps, this time on foot," said Zandra.

The meat was done so they shared it amongst them and dug the potatoes out from under the coals. They ate in silence. At the bottom of the *donga* a small stream gurgled so they had plenty of water.

"That is a lot of gold," said Johan softly. "What do you intend to do with it if you find it."

They sat quietly again for a while as this thought sunk in.

"I think we should give it to the Transvaal Republic," said Zandra, after a long silence.

"The Transvaal Republic doesn't exist anymore," countered Johan.

"Legally, I suppose, it belongs to the new government," said Lorraine.

"Really," said Johan with disgust in his voice, "you want to give it to the *Khakis*?"

Everyone grunted and mumbled.

"Hey, we have to find it first," said Gideon.

"Yes," said Johan, "but when we do find it we had better have a plan."

"Are you suggesting we keep it?" asked Lorraine with surprise.

Johan started nodding.

"I think we should keep it," said Lorraine looking sideways at Zandra, looking for her approval.

"You realise we would be stealing form the British?" asked Gideon, looking all round, a smile on his face.

"That would be a good thing," remarked Zandra, her voice rising a bit.

"How do you think we will move it?" asked Gideon. He wasn't sure this was a good idea. "We would need ox wagons to cart it away, just as they did to start with."

"The wagons may still be there but the oxen definitely won't be," added Johan.

They were quiet again for a while. Johan added wood to the fire and Zandra stood up to pour coffee. When she sat down again, she blew on the hot coffee. Everyone was quiet.

Then, "we could bury it and come back for it later, maybe fetch a little at a time."

They were thinking it over.

"I don't have any better idea," said Johan.

Gideon nodded and glanced around at the others.

They grunted and nodded agreement.

"First, as I said before, we have to find it," said Gideon, "anyway what makes us any better than the men who stole it in the first place?"

"Well," said Zandra with a lot of heat, "you aside, those men were stealing our freedom. Who knows, the guns and ammunition that the gold was supposed to buy, could have made a difference."

Gideon clicked his tongue.

Zandra turned on him, "nobody is asking you, *Engelsman*,"

Gideon kept quiet.

"Let's try again in the morning," Johan broke the thick silence.

Gideon poured himself another mug of coffee. He sat deep in thought, careful not to stare at the flames. Where did they go wrong? What had they missed?

They knew that the wagons had passed the *drift* where the black couple had been sitting. The land was broken quite a lot with hollows. He didn't know what had caused them but they were ideal to hide a wagon but whether they were big enough to hide a wagon and a full span of oxen? He didn't think so. Besides, as far as he could remember, there were at least three wagons and they were heavy wagons. Gideon didn't know this area very well but he tried to imagine what he would do if he had organised the theft.

That brought him to another thought. Why would patriotic Boers do such a thing? It was no wonder that they suspected him. Although he was a Boer at heart, having been born on the land, he was also from foreign blood and as far as the other Boers were concerned, an *Engelsman*, as Zandra had said.

Gideon woke suddenly. He hadn't felt himself dozing off. It was very dark with the moon in its first quarter. The fire had burned down to coals. Who was supposed to be on watch? The bush was too quiet, he didn't like it, something was wrong. He slowly moved his hand to his rifle, trying to open his eyes as wide as possible, trying to see in the dark. Surely the horses would have made a noise if a cat was close and where was Geel?

All of a sudden, all hell broke loose. A high pitched, angry growl from Geel as he leapt across the clearing in front of Gideon sending grit into Gideon's face. It was too dark to see clearly as Gideon rolled upright, first thinking a leopard was in the camp but then a rifle blew flame from the side and in the deafening blast, he realised that they were under attack. A blood-curdling scream turned into a gurgle just before another rifle blossomed right beside Gideon's ear. After that he was totally deaf. Gideon rolled again, feeling really stupid. He couldn't see anything and now he couldn't hear anything. Grit was scratching in his eye as he rolled as far as he could before coming up against a tree stump. Guns were blazing now with bullets zipping through the air above him.

In the light of the flashes and seeing where they came from, Gideon worked out that there were five attackers in the bush around them. The attackers must be really stupid. They should have wiped out the whole camp with one volley of rifle-fire. Gideon could hear Geel dashing about, growling and giving short barks but then there was a shot and he gave two short yelps and was quiet. A rifle flashed in the bush, followed immediately by a shot from the camp and a thrashing around that indicated someone down out there.

It all went quiet apart from the ringing in his ears, Gideon tried not to rub his eye. After a few more minutes of stillness he heard Johan call out. Immediately a rifle shot snapped in the bush followed by a shot from the camp. Gideon peered around the stump but couldn't see anything. The bush was just vague silhouettes. The sky was full of stars and the thin sliver of a moon didn't give much light. He looked back toward the camp and could make out the embers of the dying fire surrounded by rocks. He thought he saw movement there.

Gideon started rolling again, "Johan," he called while he was rolling.

No shot came. The bush was quiet again.

"Gideon?" came a call to his left. Quiet again.
After a few minutes he heard Zandra, "I think they
are gone," then, "Lorraine, are you alright?"
"Hurt," called Lorraine.
Gideon's heart froze. He stood into a crouch and
moved toward where he had heard her voice.
He nearly fell over her. "Careful," she said.
Gideon knelt beside her, "where?" he asked.
"Don't you go feeling around!" she snapped at him.
He jerked his hands back.
"Mind out the way," said Zandra behind him.

He stepped aside. While he stood there feeling like an
idiot, he used the collar of his shirt to ease the dirt
from the corner of his eye. Johan was throwing
branches onto the fire. He had fed it with twigs and
had a blaze going. They skirted the clearing, calling
to Geel. Johan found him. Gideon reached him as he
lifted the dog and carried him into the light of the fire.
His head hung limp, lifeless. They knelt on each side
of him. Johan put his ear to the dog's chest.

"Nothing," he said as he started rubbing Geel's chest. Gideon put his hand on the dog's head and it came away wet with blood. They left him there as they moved toward the girls.

"A bullet must have cut a groove in her left arm," said Zandra, "boil some water and I'll clean it."

By the time they had things sorted out, the grey morning light was creeping in. The birds were waking and making a terrific noise in a Maroela tree nearby.

"The horses are gone," said Johan from where he was standing.

He wandered down the stream bed, looking for spoor.

"Keep an eye open for honey," called Zandra.

Gideon searched the bush, trying to figure out what had happened. He found all five, dressed like Boers, their clothes not more than rags. One of them was soaked in blood, his throat ripped out. Geel had done his bit. Gideon dragged each of them to the fire and lay them in a row. One was very young, Gideon guessed about thirteen or fourteen. Another had a white beard and creased face. Maybe this was a family.

It was light now. Johan came up the *donga*, leading their horses and another five besides. Gideon helped him tie them up. One of the horses had a smaller saddle and had a red rag tied to the saddle-bag. Gideon's heart felt heavy as he loosened the bag and pulled out the youngster's clean shirt, neatly rolled. A folded paper fell to the ground. Gideon's throat pulled tight, anticipating what he would find. There were only a few words in Dutch;

 'May God go with you my beautiful boy, I love you a lot, Ma.'

Gideon walked over to the boy's body and carefully pushed the note into the boy's shirt pocket. He supposed that one of the dead men was the boy's father. He couldn't fathom out why this raggy band had attacked the camp. They should've seen that the camp was a Boer camp. If they had just asked, Gideon was sure the girls and Johan would have shared their food. Even if they were unsure, the war was over. Maybe they didn't know that, such senseless deaths, especially the young boy.

Gideon and Johan took their time burying the five together with all their belongings. There was nothing to show who they were. They dug the graves deep so that the wild animals wouldn't dig them up and alongside them, they buried Geel. The four of them stood quietly together in front of the graves.

"Anybody want to say anything?" asked Gideon. He looked over at Johan.

Johan swallowed as he shook his head and looked away. Both girls sobbed softly.

They sat around, none of them wanting to be the first to move away.

"Who started the shooting?" Gideon asked, looking around at them.

Zandra shrugged, Lorraine just stared ahead and Johan shook his head.

Gideon looked down and scratched in the dirt with a twig.

"We should've had someone on watch," said Johan, "why didn't we have someone on watch?"

"It wouldn't have made any difference," said Zandra, "I woke up just before the shooting started and didn't see or hear anything. Even Geel was caught off guard."

"They were very quiet," admitted Gideon.

"For Boers, they were very poor shots. Maybe they didn't mean to kill us," said Johan.

"Oh don't say that," said Lorraine with a half sob, "I don't want to think that we killed them for nothing."

"No, no," countered Gideon, "don't ever forget that they attacked us."

They sat awhile longer before getting up, one by one and swinging into the saddle. They turned again toward Pienaar's River siding leading the other five horses. They left the spare horses at a stable near to the siding. They told the stable owner that they had found the horses wandering around the bush, maybe someday, someone would come looking for them. There was no hotel nearby. The mongrel was still lying on the platform when the four of them dismounted in front of the wood and iron building on the platform. He lifted his mangy head and stared at them for a short while before dropping his chin onto his forepaws again. A man was sitting at a table inside the building. The table was being used as a desk. It had wire baskets on the one end with paper-work jutting out of them. He looked up as they walked in but waited for them to speak.

"Good afternoon *Oom*," Gideon greeted him in Afrikaans.

The man stood and came around the table with his hand outstretched for a hand-shake.

"Gideon Barron," Gideon introduced himself.

"Kurt Gimmel," the man introduced himself, "what can I do for you?" he asked in Afrikaans but with a heavy German accent.

Gideon introduced the others.

"*Oom,*" said Gideon, "we are looking for accommodation for one night."

Kurt steered him to the door and pointed across the rails, about a hundred yards down the track to a white painted house with a green roof.

"*Tannie* Betty takes in overnighters," he said, "and she is a very good cook."

They all said their thank-you's and moved off across the tracks in the general direction of the house.

"Why do we need accommodation," said Lorraine, as soon as they were far enough away to be out of hearing to Kurt.

"Well, I for one need a decent bath," said Gideon, he was going to say 'and a good meal' but he thought the girls may take that to mean they couldn't cook.

As they came closer to the house Lorraine said, "I suppose I wouldn't mind a meal that I haven't cooked myself."

Zandra grunted and Johan made a strange noise.

"It's no use asking anything about the gold," said Johan as they walked up the dusty street to the house. Nobody added anything.

They tied the horses to the rail and walked up the few wooden steps onto the veranda. The veranda was swept clean. A wooden bench stood to one side of an open front door. A swing screen door was closed so Zandra rang a brass bell hanging to one side. The brass was also polished, a good sign.

A middle-aged woman walked up the passage toward them, "come in, come in," she said opening the screen door.

Gideon stood with his hat in hand. He could smell food cooking, smelt like lamb stew. There was also a slight smell of coffee in there somewhere. He let the women go in ahead of him, looking forward to a night of luxury.

The inevitable result of war is death.

Malan

CHAPTER 6

Bertus stepped down off the veranda of the general store in Elandsfontein and strode toward the barn where his horse was being kept. His name was actually Albertus but nobody had called him that since his mother had died during the drought of '98. Drought came often to this part of the world and when it did all the farmers suffered. It meant that they had to scrounge to stay alive. No *mielies* to take to the farmer's co-op meant they had no money for coffee or sugar or proper medicine. There was always the herbal medicine that the old people used but they hadn't saved his mother.

Anyway, that was all something of the past for him now. The war had taken his father and his brother, Sybrand. The farm was still there but the cattle had been slaughtered by the British to feed their troops. They hadn't burnt the house down because they had been using it for a local headquarters. Bertus didn't feel like going back to it. All the family, personal stuff had been cleared out so it was almost as if they had wiped out all the memories.

Now that the war was over, he could go and do whatever he felt like doing and now with his share of the gold, the world was open to him. Natal and the Cape were British held so he didn't want to go walking around down there weighted down with stolen gold. Mozambique was a good option with an open port at Delegoa Bay. Bertus had heard of some Americans who were willing to pay good money for gold bullion. His friend, Hannes, had told him that an American ship captain, who frequented Delegoa Bay, had bought gold from him on previous occasions. He couldn't understand why Hannes had gone off with those three other men. Bertus and Hannes had always been friends but now, just because one of the others wanted to pick up his girl-friend in Naboomspruit, Hannes had ridden off with them without making proper arrangements about where and when they were supposed to meet up.

It had been nearly two months since they had left. Bertus knew that they hadn't fetched the gold without him because he knew where the gold was. The Elands River had come down in flood twice since they had left. He thought about it as he crossed the drift. The river was back to normal now, just a narrow stream. Over the years the river had washed a slash in the landscape and it was in there that they had hidden the wagons of gold and the oxen that night. His girl-friend was waiting for him in the barn. Well not really a girl-friend in the romantic sense. He had known Elsie all his life. They had gone to the farm school together and now she had come back from the concentration camp in Vereeniging, they had just naturally started just going together again. She was harder now though. Bertus wasn't sure if he liked that in a woman.

She handed him the reins of his mare and they walked back to the store to pick up the supplies that Bertus had bought. Both their horses were carrying bags behind their saddles for the provisions. Not big enough to carry gold though. They had decided to buy a cart and horses in Nelspruit to load Bertus' share of the gold. Elsie was adamant that they should only take a fair share but they had waited long enough for Hannes to come back.

"Hannes and his friends could get their share whenever they wished," Elsie had said to Bertus, "but Bertus was entitled to take his fair share."

Hannes had said they wouldn't be long. Only a few days, he had said. Well the time had come. Bertus had told Elsie that they may climb on a boat going to Madagascar or they may even be able to hitch a ride on that American boat, the Dorethea, Elsie thought she remembered Bertus saying one night when they had finished off a bottle of peach brandy that they had made a month earlier.

They swung into the saddle, Elsie wearing men's trousers and riding straddle as a lot of young women were these days. It felt strange to leave Elandsfontein again, each of them knowing that this time they wouldn't be coming back but there was nothing for them here anymore except empty farmhouses. They forded the drift again and Bertus thought back to the night they had stolen Paul Kruger's gold. It hadn't been too long ago but before Elsie had arrived home. Her mother had died in the concentration camp. Some of the women had gone on a hunger strike. When they had become weak and frail, the British had tried to force feed them but it hadn't worked. They had died. Elsie had tried to persuade her mother to eat but she wouldn't.

Bertus and Hannes hadn't planned this robbery. It had just fallen into place. They had volunteered to load ammunition. It had started off just fine. General Beyers himself had ridden with them to Pienaar's River. He had left Veldkornet Viljoen in charge. Even after General Beyers had ridden away things had gone pretty well.

Six men from another commando had joined them on the ride in. Bertus, for one, was glad of the extra help but he could see that some of the other men were not happy. He heard one of his group snarl at one of them but couldn't hear what was said. He only heard

115

Clarence tell them where they were going. When Clarence and Hannes walked their horses forward to scout the siding, Bertus saw some of the others exchanging glances but didn't know why.

It didn't take them long. They were soon back. They moved forward and Bertus heard them confirming that the wagons were ready at the siding.

Viljoen motioned them forward but Clarence and some of the others hung back as the rest moved through the bush out to the clearing on either side of the track and siding. Three ox-wagons were standing by at the bottom of the siding.

"Come men," Viljoen called, "we need to move this load before the *Khakies* upset things."

They dismounted at a hitchrail near a green, wood and iron building.

Once they started loading the boxes from the siding onto the wagons, it was obvious that this wasn't ammunition. The boxes were far too heavy.

Bertus whispered to Hannes, "what is going on? These boxes are not carrying ammunition."

"Just keep your head down and keep loading," answered Hannes in a whisper.

Two men struggled to handle one box.

"It's gold," said Hannes.

Just then they heard Viljoen confirm that it was gold, meant to pay for arms and ammunition from Holland and Germany.

"Ag no," grunted Hannes, "that's going to make it harder."

Bertus was confused. He didn't understand what was happening. He tried to get Hannes to talk again but Hannes just waved him off. Once a few of the wagons were full and were pulled away, Hannes motioned him closer to pick up another box.

"Just be ready when I give you the signal," he said.

"For what," Bertus asked, still confused.

Hannes gave him a look as if to say, 'how stupid can you be.'

Bertus felt his face burn. Why did Hannes always make him feel bad? He didn't know why he stayed friends with Hannes. It had been this way all their lives. He knew he was cleverer than Hannes but Hannes always managed to make Bertus feel inferior.

When they stopped for a drink, Bertus tried to ask him again but Hannes waved him off again. At that point Bertus would have gladly put a bullet in the back of Hannes' head. He knew though that as soon as he cooled down, he would do exactly as Hannes asked.

They loaded into the evening. Bertus searched his soul. He had to make an effort to get away from Hannes but it was difficult. He always felt comfortable when he was with Hannes. Not that he had any homosexual feelings toward him. Bertus shuddered at the thought. Hannes had even bullied Bertus in the early years at farm school. Elsie had also tried to get him to make friends with other boys but he had always resisted.

Bertus' thoughts were interrupted by a shot and shouting and Viljoen urged them to move faster. "*Khakis* are coming," said Hannes as they swung another case up onto the wagon.

The powerful light beam of a loco cut through the bush as it took a curve and then lit up the track as it straightened out.

"Keep close," shouted Hannes to Bertus as they mounted.

Bullets zipped through the air above them and Hannes pulled his horse around to make sure that Bertus was up and running and, of course, Bertus felt that old bond between them.

They galloped after the wagons. Some men had stayed to form a rear guard but Hannes motioned Bertus forward. As they reached the bush line Bertus saw four others waiting for them. A shot rang out right next to him but he put his heels in and kept going. When he looked back, he noticed that Viljoen wasn't with them. When he looked back toward the battle, he saw, in the light of the loco, someone bending over a man on the ground.

They drove the oxen hard through the night. They were moving east and Bertus was satisfied with that because it was in the general direction of Mozambique and Delegoa Bay. By daybreak they had reached the Elands River. They drove the wagons into the river bed and stopped. Bertus noticed that there were only six riders. Things didn't seem right.

"What is going on?" he asked as he dismounted next to Hannes.

Hannes motioned him to come along.

They left the horses and joined the others. They were passing water-bottles and sticks of biltong around. Hannes turned to him, "we are taking the gold," he said.

Bertus' jaw dropped as he quickly looked around at the others. They all just glanced at him and carried on with what they were doing.

"Are you mad?" he asked in shock, "this is Kruger's gold. You will be shot. Besides," he went on, "this is supposed to buy ammunition for the Republic."

Hannes was quiet for a few minutes, waiting for Bertus to calm down. "The war is over, boet," he said softly, "we can't win. The Brits are pumping men into this country and there are already talks of us negotiating for peace."

"I will fight to the death," spluttered Bertus vehemently.

Hannes clicked his tongue, "don't be stupid," he said, still softly, "what are you going to shoot when the bullets are finished. What this gold can buy won't last another six months. Our women are all in concentration camps now so we have no way of getting food from the farms. Use your head. We are taking this gold for ourselves for when the war ends. Without it we will have nothing. The Brits have even taken our livestock to feed their troops."

Bertus was quiet for a few minutes, thinking hard. He knew that Hannes was doing him a favour by including him in the group but Hannes would have done nothing less. He always looked after Bertus. "What then and how?" he eventually asked, turning to Hannes.

"We know an American who will buy the gold from us. Not for its full value of course but enough to make us all rich. Then you can decide where you want to go from there.

"What are you going to do?" he asked Hannes, softly now.

"Me?" he asked, "I am not sure yet. I may go to Madagascar or America, even maybe Argentina but I am not staying here under British rule again. If you want to come with me, you can. I might even take Suzi with me. I'll have enough money to buy a ticket for her on a ship too."

Bertus nodded but he didn't like the idea of Suzi going with them. Not that he was jealous but Hannes would be waltzing around with Suzi while he sat around like an extra *disselboom* on an oxwagon. Bertus nodded again and Hannes clapped him on the shoulder before turning away to join the others. They even made a fire that night for cooking. Not too big but the low river bed sheltered them from the eyes of any followers. They were close enough to Elandsfontein for Bertus and Hannes to go to their farms but Hannes said that they must leave again at daybreak. It was a long ride to Delegoa Bay and the port of Lorenzo Marques. With the wagons it was going to take at least a week.

A storm had passed them by that afternoon. Hopefully it had washed their spoor away. The smell of wet veld still hung in the air. After eating grilled meat and potatoes for supper and a second cup of black coffee, Bertus lay on his blanket and thought about going with Hannes. He didn't really want to leave Africa but if this country fell to British rule again, it wouldn't be his country anymore. The Brits would be telling them what they could and couldn't do and lording over the Boers.

If Hannes was going to take Suzi with him then maybe Bertus should take a girl too but he didn't really have a girlfriend. There was Elsie; not really his girlfriend and he didn't know if she would go with him. Maybe she had a boyfriend that he didn't know about and where would they go, just follow Hannes he supposed. It was always easier just to follow Hannes. Elsie was pretty enough, a bit headstrong though. She had laid a strip into him a few times when they were younger if she didn't get her way or if she thought that he was doing something stupid. He fell asleep thinking of distant horizons and Elsie by his side.

Hannes kicked him awake, "if you want coffee, you had better move," the sky in the east was getting lighter. Someone had gotten up early to cook *slappap* and they even had milk to pour over it. Bertus poured a little milk in his coffee, a bit of a luxury.

They struggled to get the oxen and wagons out of the river-bed so that tempers were wearing thin by the time they were finally on their way moving east in a row, wagon behind wagon. Bertus rode wide, pretending to watch for Brits but secretly he just wanted to keep out of the dust. If anybody had looked west that morning and looked carefully, they would've seen the dust cloud that rose over the Flats. Even though it had rained the previous afternoon, the dry land had soaked up all the water. Good for the bush though and some streams may be running so the animals were happy.

The weaver birds had built their nests fairly low on the branches. They seemed to know, if heavy rains were coming, they would build their enormous community nests higher up in the tree.
The going was easy for the oxen despite the heavy load they were pulling. They made good time. Hannes

called Bertus in just after noon. It was no use trying to keep quiet. They were pulling heavy loads and had to keep urging the oxen forward with shouts and the long bullwhips cracking overhead. Usually they would use young black boys to walk in front, leading the oxen but with what they were doing, they had to do the leading themselves. Bertus had no doubt that he would be called upon to do his share.

There was only water to drink and biltong and dried peaches were handed around to eat in the saddle. The oxen and horses were watered first. They were soon on the move again.

I am homesick for a place
I am not sure even exists
One where my heart is full
My body loved
And my soul understood
Unknown

CHAPTER 7

It took them three days of hard driving to arrive just north of Nelspruit at a junction in the river, a place called Rolle. By this time tempers were flaring often. Bertus tried to stay out of it but it wasn't easy. Hannes always stuck up for him and Bertus knew that the two of them could take on the rest of these *jafles* any day but they needed each other to get this gold to the coast.

In front of them lay the Drakensburg mountains, not easy to cross but they knew of a pass downstream of the Crocodile River. They would need to scout the route though. The sun was touching the foothills behind them when they pulled the oxen to a stop on the banks of a river bed. One of the ox leaders dropped the lead and walked forward onto the sand. It was obvious to all of them that the sand was too soft for wagon wheels to be pulled through.

Jakes, who now fancied himself the leader of the group, said they should camp on the riverbank for the night and figure out what to do. Even though Bertus knew this was the right thing to do, he was reluctant just on principal. He didn't say anything and saw that Hannes had relented anyway. Sitting and eating around the fire that night, the atmosphere was a bit tense.

It was soon after the meal that Jakes and Pieter started arguing. That was always the trouble with the Boers, everyone wanted to be the leader. The Great Trek was a good example of that. That is why there wasn't one great trek but many, because the different groups couldn't agree where to go or when to go. Anyway, it became a real humdinger.

"I think we should make skids to the wheels as soon as daybreaks," announced Jakes.

Bertus was just about to nod when Pieter cut in, "I think we should go downstream and find a *drift* with a stony bottom."

"Alright Pieter," answered Jakes, "you ride downstream to look for one and in the meantime the rest of us will start making skids."

Bertus thought that was a reasonable plan but Pieter jumped to his feet, "are you telling me what to do?" he shouted venomously.

Jakes was silent for a few seconds, "calm down, Pieter, let's wait till morning and then discuss it. I think we are all tired and need a sleep."

Bertus thought the 'calm down' was the wrong thing for Jakes to say but he couldn't understand why Pieter was so upset.

"Don't tell me to calm down and I am not tired," Pieter was shouting and spitting bullets now, "why do you think you are leader all of a sudden?"

Bertus agreed with that but this was a useless argument.

"Do what you like," said Jakes softly, "I am going to sleep." With that he turned his back on Pieter and started getting his blanked ready to sleep.

"Don't turn your back on me!" shouted Pieter and started bringing his rifle up.

"Uh, uh," said Hannes softly and came to his feet in front of Pieter.

"Get out of my way!" shouted Pieter, his rifle already on his hip.

Bertus also stood up next to Hannes and held his hand up, showing Pieter to stop.

There were a few tense moments before Pieter turned on his heel and marched off away from the fire.

It took a while for the rest of them to calm down. The fire was burning low when the last one pulled his blanked over his shoulder. Pieter was still out in the dark when Bertus fell asleep.

They woke to the early light of dawn and went about the business of making skids for the wagon wheels. Two of the burgers stirred up the fire and started cooking *mielie* meal and boiling water for coffee. Those working on the wagons, broke away one by one to eat the *pap* and *boerewors* and have a few cups of coffee.

As they finished fixing the skids on a wagon, they would drag it across the river bed. It wasn't very wide, only about twenty-five yards with a narrow stream meandering down the middle but the oxen struggled amid a lot of shouting and bull-whipping above their heads. The sand was loose and deep; even the horses had a heavy going of it. It was getting on for a sweltering midday when Pieter came bursting through the bush toward them.

"Brits!" he said urgently, "heading in this direction."
"How far?" asked Hannes.
"About a half hour up the valley between the mountains."
Men scrambled for their shirts that had been discarded on the bank, their saddles thrown across their horse's rumps and rifles and bandoliers lifted as they mounted.
Jakes took charge and this time everyone listened to him, "Pieter and Hannes!" he shouted, "create a diversion. Try to lead them away from here. The rest of you, drag that last wagon across as it is.!"

Everyone jumped into action. Nobody questioned his authority, not even Pieter. One of the men with the front two wagons turned back. They had taken the skids off the wheels and had started hauling the wagons further up the next ridge. The road curved along the river-side, around a natural bend.

"Bertus!" Jakes shouted, "go tell those men to keep going, all the way to the sea."

Bertus was already in the saddle and he jumped his horse forward toward the other side of the river. When the man who had turned around, saw him he guessed what needed to be done. He waved to Bertus, spun his horse around and galloped out toward the front wagons. When Bertus turned, a grim sight met his eyes. Already the last wagon was starting to sink into the sand. The whips cracked above the oxen. The oxen bellowed, straining against the leather thongs, their thick, sweaty necks pushing against the yokes. They managed to drag that wagon up to the stream, they were even standing over it but couldn't go any further. They were straining and pulling but to no avail.

"Outspan, outspan, get the oxen away!" shouted Jakes.

The wheels were up to their axels and couldn't be budged. As the oxen were driven away, the first flat, sharp shots rang out from the Mausers of Pieter and Hannes. It took only a few seconds before they were answered by the heavier crack of the Lee-Metfords of the British.

"Take cover behind the wagon!" shouted Jakes, "don't let them take it."

Bertus felt the now familiar pump of adrenaline through his body. The feeling had become his friend, giving him extra speed and strength in times of trouble. His feet came out of the stirrups, his stomach guiding him off the horse. He hit the ground running, at the same time slapping his horse's rump, getting it moving toward the other bank and out of harm's way. He dived into the sand, taking up position under the *disselboom* in the front of the wagon. He tried to calm himself in order to shoot straight, lying, watching the bank where the road came down to the river-bed.

Bertus could hear the rifles of Pieter and Hannes up the valley toward the Drakensberg but they didn't seem to be moving away. They weren't drawing the British away. It didn't take long before the shooting broke off completely, Bertus hoped that Hannes was alright. Sometimes he really hated him but he was like a brother. The sound of thundering hooves brought him back to the present. A cloud of dust was being kicked up on the road and a party of riders came into view. Definitely British soldiers, not wearing the old red uniforms. They had learnt their lesson the first time around when they were hammered at The Hill of Doves, *Amajuba*. Now they wore khaki, hence the name *Khakis*.

The Brits were expecting something but they didn't know what. They pulled their horses up in a bunch on the river bank, taken a bit by surprise at what they were seeing, they meuled around for half a minute, dust billowing up in front of them.
"*Vuur,*" screamed Jakes and the Boer Mausers thundered, cutting the soldiers down before they could even see what was happening.

Bertus felt his rifle kick against his shoulder like a good friend. His right hand whipped back and forth on the bolt, putting those little babies into the chamber and sending them on their way. He tried to carefully keep the chamber out of the dust, cupping it under his left hand instead of holding the stock. He let the stock settle on his shirt that he had placed there earlier.

A few soldiers spun their horses and spurred them back up the road, only to be met by Hannes and Pieter. They didn't have a chance, 9mm slugs lifted them out of their saddles. The horses kept on going without them, the stirrups bouncing along against their rumps. The bodies lay in the road. Bertus stood up on his knees and watched Hannes walk his horse toward him and they both raised their rifles in the air in salute.

The joy didn't last long. "There is a big column of Brits about an hour away!" shouted Hannes, "heading in this direction."

"Quickly men," said Jakes earnestly, "Start burying the gold bars in the sand."

"There is an old abandoned mine shaft just around the bend," said Pieter, "I saw it as we rode up the pass."

"Alright, go, go, go," said Jakes but men were already loading bars into their saddle bags.

The horses were weighed down with the gold but they managed to take half of the gold up to the mine before Jakes called them to stop.

"It's too slow!" shouted Jakes, "bury the rest of it in the sand."

The men worked as if the devil was on his way and more than likely he was, seeing this was gold and the Brits were coming. They soon had it all buried in the sand, put horses in the yokes and, with a lot of pushing and shoving, got the wagon moving to the other side of the river bed. Men were scrambling to cover the tracks so that suspicion wouldn't be called to the position of the buried gold.

The empty wagon was dragged some way into the bush and a cliff was found to tip it over. It bounced a few times before landing in another river bed. By this time the Brits were upon them and a retreat action was started down river to draw the soldiers away from the wagons making their way to the coast. How nobody from the company of Boers was killed was nothing short of a miracle.

There must've been at least fifty soldiers, well trained too. After three years in the South African bush, these *khakis* had learnt a thing or two. Bertus was firing while turned in the saddle. He didn't think he hit anyone but it made them careful about following too close. They were chased south until sundown when the attack slowly faded until it was too dark to see and the British pulled up to let the Boers slip away in the night.

By the light of the moon Bertus and his friends carried on south until Pieter said he was sure they must be close to the Swazi border. There they stopped and made camp by the bank of a river that no-one new the name of. They were pleased with themselves. Nobody had been shot and Pieter had now come to recognise Jakes as the leader. It was under Jakes' command that they built a cooking fire and watered the horses. They were all in a jovial mood. Someone played tunes on a mouthorgan and there was much joking and laughing.

"I carved some crosses on a tree in line with the place we buried the gold," said Jakes. "As soon as things have settled down, we can come back and collect it. The wagons that have gone on to the coast will have to be hidden in Lorenco Marques until we can sell it all together. I will go there now to arrange the hiding place. The rest of you can make your way back to your farms until the time is right."

Bertus wasn't sure how far they could trust Jakes with such a large wealth of gold.

"How much do you think we will get for the gold?" Bertus asked.

"Not nearly as much as it is worth," answered Jakes, "but enough to make every one of us rich, enough to be able to start again somewhere where we don't have to listen to the English Lords."

They all laughed. Hannes seemed to be spending a lot of time with Pieter and one of the others, Bertus thought his name was Kobus but they called him

Ouboet. Bertus knew that Hannes would look after him and make sure he was given his share but he felt a bit uneasy. It left his mind as he got into the general feeling of joviality of the others. He went to sleep dreaming of the farm that he was going to buy someplace in Paradise.

Love everyone. But never sell your sword.

Paulo Coelho

CHAPTER 8

At daybreak, Jakes left for the coast. Pieter wanted to tag along and Jakes didn't feel he could refuse him. They crossed the Lebombo Mountains and moved across the coastal plain toward the sea. Jakes reckoned once they reached the sea, they could ask the locals directions to Delegoa Bay and Lorenco Marques, well they could only move north or south. Jakes had a friend at the port and he knew of an American captain who was said to be interested in this type of thing. He expected that the two wagons would move straight to the port. The two men driving those wagons could be trusted, both of them good men.

It was hot, sticky hot. Their sweat soaked their shirts. Jakes kept on taking his hat off to wipe his forehead. He was scared to leave his hat off, for fear of sunstroke and sunburn. It was hotter here than in the bushveld. He could see that Pieter was having a hard time too. Banana, paw-paw and mangoes grew wild here, more than likely planted by some Portuguese farmers a long, long time ago. It grew hotter and stickier as they drew closer to the sea but they crested a rise and sea lay before them. They stayed landward side of the dunes. Jakes knew how hot that beach sand could become. It was just past midday and that sand could burn blisters on the horse's shanks. At least along the sea-front a light breeze was blowing. The sand was white as sugar and the sea a deep blue.

They moved south. Jakes wasn't sure if they were moving in the right direction, it just felt right. They came to a small river mouth. Men, stripped to loin clothes, were throwing fishing nets in a lagoon. Jakes swung down and tasted the water of the lagoon, it tasted sweet. He let his horse bend and take a few sips.

"Are you well," he called to the men in Zulu. He was sure they were Shangaan but he didn't know any Shangaan.

They stopped work and all turned to him. One man said something to him in Portuguese but Jakes didn't know any Portuguese. Jakes looked over at Pieter, still mounted but Pieter just shrugged.

"Lorenco Marques?" said Jakes, holding his palms up, hoping that they would understand.

The man who had spoken before, babbled away in Portuguese again but then turned and pointed south down the coast.

"Thank you, thank you," said Jakes in Zulu.

He was sure that they could understand him. Shangaan and Zulu weren't so different but they just stood and stared at him. He swung up and they walked their horses through the shallow river-mouth between the lagoon and the sea.

As they worked their way south, Pieter fell in behind him. He had hardly said a word the whole day. All of a sudden, he kicked his horse forward into a gallop and charged past Jakes.

"Pieter, Pieter! What is it?" shouted Jakes but Pieter didn't look back.

Jakes galloped after Pieter for a while, calling to him but at last decide to just let him go. He was a fair way ahead by this time. He knew that Pieter didn't like him because he had taken charge of their small commando but thought he had gotten over it when he asked to go along with him to the port.

It wasn't long before Pieter was out of sight but then a few low buildings came into sight. As he rode, he came across more and more European style houses with a dirt road running along the sea front. There were no lawns here, it was too hot and the air was salty. Jakes had been here before, not too long ago to visit his friend, Anthony or Tony to his friends. He found the house quite easily and Tony was sitting on a wide veranda just off the street.

"Well, well," said Tony in English with a very heavy Portuguese accent coming out of his wicker chair, "*como esta?*"

"*Moite bein obrigado*," answered Jakes but that was as far as his Portuguese went.

Tony turned and rattled off some Portuguese toward the open front door.

They sat and drank red wine with Portuguese rolls and smoked black, thin *cigarillos*.

It was dark by the time they had caught up with all their news. They spoke English only because it was the only language that they both knew. Tony's servant girl brought out a paraffin lamp with a yellow glass to keep the mosquitoes away and they wiped all the exposed parts of their bodies with citronella oil. This was malaria country and nobody took a chance here.

The conversation finally got around to the gold.

"So, my friend, what brings you to LM?" asked Tony

"Tony, I may be able to get hold of some gold bullion," answered Jakes

"Mmm," said Tony around the mouthpiece of a pipe he had picked up off a side table and was tamping tobacco with a box of matches.

"Are you still in contact with that American captain, who you told me about?" Jakes carried on.

Tony puffed for a few minutes on his pipe, "maybe," he answered, looking sideways at Jakes.

"We'll cut you in," said Jakes.

"We, who is we?" asked Tony.

"Six friends who helped me get the gold," answered Jakes, "but there is enough for all of us."

Jakes knew that his friend was not a greedy man so he knew he would help if he could.

"I suppose the authorities mustn't know," it was a statement, not a question.

Jakes kept quiet. An answer wasn't necessary. Tony puffed away again for a few more minutes.

Finally, he took the pipe out of his mouth, "yes, I am still in contact. I did him a favour just last week, some papers he needed signing by a citizen, captain Harold Mathisson of the sloop, the Dorothea."

"Yes, that's him. Do you think he would be in the market for gold bullion?" asked Jakes.

"Everyone is in the market for gold, my friend but this one has a ship to carry it and a country to take it to." Jakes could see the interest in Tony's mannerisms now.

"By the way," Tony went on, "I am told that ships from Holland and Germany were waiting off shore here, waiting for payment for arms. Not the same gold I suppose?

Jakes kept quiet, again an answer wasn't necessary. "In the morning we will speak with the captain," Tony knocked the pipe against the heel of his boot, "the dockyards are too dangerous at night for a man who is not a sailor."

They ate a supper of rock-cod and garlic potatoes with sliced mango on the side. After an obligatory cup of black coffee, they carried on well into the night on local red wine. Jakes made sure that he didn't get too drunk, he still had Pieter to worry about and sure enough, in the early hours, he came calling. Jakes lay on the coconut coir filled mattress, looking at the moon through the window opening. A mosquito net covered his bed and it was this that saved him. For a few seconds Pieter was confused as he was caught up in the net. As the net slowed the knife slash, Jakes' revolver roared in such a confined space. Pieter was thrown back by the Webley's heavy bullet. Jakes whipped the net aside and was prepared to fire again as he swung his legs to the floor but Pieter was past caring. Jakes felt for a pulse on Pieter's neck but there was nothing. His broken heart had pumped it's last.

Tony slammed through the door, a pistol in his hand but relaxed as he saw, by the light of his storm-lantern, the limp body under Jakes' knee.

"You alright?" he asked.

"Fine," said Jakes.

"Friend of yours?" Tony asked.

"Was," answered Jakes.

It was past midnight by the time Tony's men had loaded Pieter's body onto the back of a donkey cart and had driven away to 'who knows where'.

Jakes struggled to fall asleep again. He would've thought that after three years of battle he would be used to bloodshed but taking someone's life at such close quarters always left him with remorse, even when the man had been trying to kill him.

He woke at first light as usual. He could hear activity elsewhere in the house and a cock started crowing near to his window. He pulled on his boots and went to find water to wash.

Tony was sitting at the kitchen table reading a Portuguese newspaper. His servant girl was cooking *mielie-meel* in a big pot on the coal-stove.

"They say the war is over," he said without looking up. "They are coming together to sign a peace treaty." Jakes just grunted. He was surprised though that it had happened so fast after their skirmish at Pienaars River. Those soldiers who had attacked them on the river bed couldn't have known about it.

They ate porridge and drank a few cups of coffee before setting off on Tony's horse cart to the docks. The cart was a Spider and made good time. The land was flat, the roads were hard packed earth. Tropical fruit trees lined the street. The smell of the sea was strong. The tide was out so the Dorothea sat low in the docks, a beautiful ship, although Jakes knew very little about ships. Men were loading, what looked like supplies. A crane was swinging big bales of something into the middle of the ship.

When Tony pulled the cart to a halt alongside, he nodded toward a man standing on a landing high up on the ship.

"The captain," said Tony softly.

The man started moving toward them so Tony motioned Jakes to wait. It took the captain a few minutes to reach them. He had to move to the middle of the ship where the walkway was down onto the dockside. He wore wide-brimmed dirty white hat, khaki shirt and trousers.

Tony and Jakes slowly moved forward to meet him.

"Tony my friend," he said in English with a twangy accent, as he stretched out a hand.

"Captain," Tony acknowledged and shook his hand, "this is my friend Jakes," he turned toward Jakes.

"Jakes, this is captain Harold Mathisson."

"My friends call me Captain," said Mathisson.

They shook hands. The Captain motioned them to follow him, away from the hustle and bustle of the activities. He pointed to a *cantina* just outside the dock area. They sat down at a table and chairs under an awning in front of the *cantina* and a young black girl took their order for coffee.

"Good to see you Tony," said the captain, "did you come down to see me? If so, you are lucky. I am sailing for my home port in the morning."

Tony told him about the gold.

The captain laughed, "I have already loaded gold bullion. You are not the only one selling gold at the end of this war of yours. I am still always in the market for more though. Two wagons are a lot of gold for me to pay for though."

He stirred sugar into his coffee, looking thoughtful. "This may be fate. I have an idea that may suit us both." He handed the sugar to Jakes who shook his head but passed it on to Tony. Tony poured milk and sugar into his coffee.

"I was sold a load of blank gold coins. I suppose in all the rush there was no time for minting. I will pay you in coin."

Jakes scowled. Tony put a restraining hand on Jakes' forearm. They both stayed silent and waited for the captain to speak again.

"I really don't have anything else to pay you with except a promissory note but then you would have to wait at least six months before I dock here again."

"How much coin do you have?" asked Jakes gruffly.

"Not nearly the true value of two wagons of bullion," answered the captain.

They were all quiet for a while, sipping their coffee. This wasn't the outcome that Jakes was hoping for but he realised that, under the circumstances he couldn't hope for much more.

"Your friend Tony knows me very well and that I am a man of honour," the captain carried on. "What I can do is give you as much coin as I have after I keep some back for my men," he held up his hand as Jakes started to say something, "I will also give you a promissory note for an agreed amount after I see the wagons."

Jakes glanced at Tony. Tony cocked his head to one side and pursed his lips and then nodded.

"I think you can trust him," Tony said, "and with that trust I think it is a good deal."

Jakes nodded and stuck out his hand. The captain took it. Jakes rode to the edge of town where he knew his men were holding the wagons. He had enough coin with him to keep the men happy. He told them where the sloop was docked.

Jakes left immediately for home and was across the Lebombo Mountains by nightfall. He was driving a light wagon pulled by two mules, his horse tied behind. He stopped on the banks of the Crocodile River. Before it was fully dark his camp was hailed from the shadows. He stood, his rifle in his left hand, a round in the chamber.

"Come on in," he called in Afrikaans.

He wasn't too worried. They wouldn't have called if they meant him harm. The gold bags were covered with a canvas sheet in the wagon, the mules grazing in a little grassy slope, far enough away from the river and crocodiles.

A man, woman and young girl came into the camp.

"Climb down," said Jakes.

The man looked understandably tense; he was bringing two females into a stranger's camp. Jakes placed his rifle on the ground to show no hostility but close enough to hand. He offered them grilled meat and coffee, that was all he had. They introduced themselves as the Coetzee family.

"The khakis have told us we must sign allegiance to the queen or leave, so we are leaving," said the man, Hendrik Coetzee.

"What about your farm?" asked Jakes.

"Burnt to nothing," answered Hendrik, "we are catching a steam ship to Madagascar."

"Is that farming country?" asked Jakes.

"So I have been told," answered Hendrik, "but anything is better than staying under the British thumb."

They spoke about farming until late. Jakes noticed that their clothes were almost rags.

"Do you have money to start again?" asked Jakes.

"No, we will have to work as labourers until we can afford to buy a small piece of land. Many Boers are going."

Jakes went to sleep thinking of this.

At daybreak Jakes was spanning the mules when the family woke. Jakes tipped his hat to the ladies.

"There is biltong and dry peaches in that bag, I'm sorry that's all I have," Jakes pointed to a bag on the ground near the fire. "there is coffee on the fire."

"*Ag baie dankie meneer*, thank you very much," said the woman, close to tears.

"May God bless you," said the man.

Jakes just nodded and slapped the reins.

He drove the cart upstream until he came to a shallow widening of the river. He shot an Impala soon after and threw it in the wagon to butcher later. All his meat had been left behind with the family. He picked monkey-apples and wild fig. Around noon he stopped to fry some eggs that Tony had given him and boiled water for coffee. He felt good when he thought of the gold in that bag he had left with the family.

He managed to get to Rollo by noon the next day. With a wagon full of gold coin, it had taken him longer that he had thought. He found the site of the bullion burial easily enough but decided to split the wagon load between the river bed and the old abandoned mine shaft. He dug a hole in the sand and stopped to rest. It was while sitting in the sand, next to the stream that he started thinking. What was he going back for? Who was waiting for him back there? The answers were simple, nothing and no-one. Dare he ask God's opinion after stealing this gold in the first place. He decided to just speak to God, not really a prayer, just speaking like he would to his dead mother. Not that he expected to get an answer from his dead mother but maybe God would give him some indication.

Well after speaking and getting no answer, he finished burying half the coin and carting the other half to the mine shaft. This mine shaft was tunnelled into the side of a mountain and was propped with timber. It didn't look too safe. He could see evidence of small rock-falls further back in the shaft. Night was coming on so he camped in front of the shaft, too scared to actually camp inside the shaft.

After cooking some of the Impala, he sliced the rest into strips and salted the strips and hung the strips in the entrance to the shaft. Maybe he would find some herbs down near the river to dust on the strips. He ate his meat and drank a few cups of coffee black, no sugar, then settled back to think.

He had left one of the promissory notes with Tony with an agreement with the captain to pay Tony in case Jakes didn't make it back. So he owed Tony nothing. He had nothing to go back to in Elandsfontein except a burnt down farm house and burnt lands. The other men knew where the gold was so they could come and fetch their share at any time. If they had any sense, they would wait awhile before trying to get rid of it.

He was thinking about what Coetzee had said. He liked the idea of making a fresh start. He didn't look forward to being subject to the British, although in some ways he thought, one government was as bad as another. He wondered what Madagascar was like. He had enough gold coin to bide his time and look around there.

The next morning he loaded what he could on his horse without overloading him and took the rest as deep into the shaft as he felt comfortable with. Maybe God had helped him make up his mind.

He was back in Mozambique by nightfall and caught up with the Coetzee family entering Lorenco Marques.

You will never reach your destination
If you stop to throw stones at every dog that barks
Winston Churchill

CHAPTER 9

Bertus trailed behind the others on the way back to Elandsfontein. Even without the wagons, it took them well into the following day to reach the *dorpie*. It wasn't even a proper village, just a trading store, a barn where horses were stabled and a blacksmith. Of course, there were the houses belonging to the people who worked in these establishments, not the blacks, the blacks lived outside the village. A market garden down by the river was run by an old Portuguese couple.

They all stopped at the trading store and sat at a long table that the Indian owner had put out on the veranda. They spoke softly when they spoke of the gold. There weren't many customers at the store but they were all discussing the peace treaty and the end of the war. Nobody was saying anything about any missing gold. Bertus and Hannes knew most of the people who were coming and going and exchanged small talk, mainly about who had arrived back from the war. It was still too soon to know who had died. That would take a few weeks for men to drift in and woman to arrive back from the concentration camps.

"Are we waiting for Jakes and Pieter?" asked Hannes, when they were finally seated with strong farm coffee. At least they had milk and sugar now.

The other three men all shook their heads.

"I say we should spend a few days with our families," said Landsman, a big farmer with a thick, full beard. "Give it about a week or so for things to calm down and then return to Rollo."

All except Bertus agreed. Bertus didn't agree because he didn't have any family. He kept quiet, no use arguing against the majority. He had Elsie; not family but he had known her all his life. He needed to talk to her anyway. He had never had a girl-friend except Elsie. She wasn't beautiful but not ugly and she could ride and shoot. The best thing about her was that

Bertus had a faint suspicion that she was in love with him. It made him hot when he thought of it.

The other four of them, including Hannes were going to ride to Naboom. Why Hannes had to go, Bertus couldn't figure out. He didn't have anyone in Naboom and Bertus had a bad feeling about Naboom. One of them, a German by the name of Kurst, seemed to be talking too much about the Gold. Bertus couldn't help thinking that too much talk could bring them bad luck.

When they all broke up, Bertus headed out to his farm, as much as was left of the farm. He made camp a little way from the house. The house was empty; the Brits must have pulled out when they heard that war was over. That night he lay listening to the Guinea fowl until they settled down in the trees and then to the jackals calling to each other. He felt a bit stupid; he was a grown man but he missed his family so much.

The next morning, he stood looking at the farm house while he drank his coffee. He couldn't get himself to go in. He walked down to the barn. It was cool in the barn and memories came flooding back. A snake slithered into hiding, a good hunting ground with all the mice around. He and Elsie would lie down under the cows and squeeze milk straight from the teat into the mouth. He felt his throat tightening so he quickly walked out. He swung into the saddle and headed toward Elsie's place about five miles away.

That was over two weeks ago, now he and Elsie were going to fetch some gold. They forded the Elands River with saddle bags full of provisions. Bertus had enough gold coin to buy a wagon in Nelspruit so they headed a little south of east. Bertus had heard at the General Store that the British troops were all headed for Durban and Cape Town to be shipped back to England. England must be a very big place to be able to hold all those soldiers, bigger than the Transvaal and the Free State put together, he thought. Anyway, he was sure that they wouldn't come across any troops in the direction he and Elsie were travelling.

The first night they camped next to a stream. Elsie was a good cook, even over a camp fire. After eating they sat shoulder to shoulder drinking coffee staring into the fire. That in itself was a bad thing because it made them vulnerable. If they had to look away from the fire, they would only see big red blotches but they felt safe and comfortable. Sitting shoulder to shoulder felt like the most natural thing in the world.

The next morning at first light they moved east, there was no hurry. Bertus was even hoping that Hannes and friends would catch up to them before he and Elsie reached the gold. That way they would help to recover the gold. Bertus didn't fancy doing the digging himself. Of course, Elsie would help him but he would rather have the others there. Landsman was big and powerful, not very bright but he could lift heavy things. That German was good company too, he had some good stories to tell.

It took them two days to reach Nelspruit, actually quite good time. The blacksmith didn't have any wagons or carts for sale but he told them of a farmer just north of town where they might get a good deal. They decided to have something to eat at the Nelspruit hotel. The food was good but there were four men who took too much notice of Elsie. Bertus wasn't jealous but he felt uncomfortable. He could see that Elsie also felt uncomfortable.

They finished up and road out of town, heading north. They found the farm just as the sun was going down. The farmer was sitting on his veranda; it was that time of day when the man of the house would sit on the veranda drinking coffee, waiting to be called in for supper. He stepped off the veranda as Bertus and Elsie swung down.

"Van Zyl," the farmer gave his surname as greeting. He held out his hand. He was shorter than Bertus and older so Hannes and Elsie addressed him as *Oom*, Uncle. They had decided to give false names but when Hannes shook the man's hand, he gave his right name. Elsie gave him a sideways glance before doing the same. They told him what they were after.

"*Kom*," he said and motioned them to follow him.

His barn seemed to be full of wagons and carts. It was dark in the barn and Van Zyl stopped just inside the door.

"No, no," he said, "could I persuade you to stay the night? It's too dark to choose a wagon in this light." He was looking at Bertus but Bertus made sure by a nod from Elsie before he nodded to Van Zyl.

"Thank you Oom," he said.

"Come in and meet my wife," Van Zyl said.

They walked into the kitchen to see a woman with grey hair standing in front of the coal stove. She was wearing a floral apron over a dark grey dress. She seemed pleased to see them when her husband introduced them. She dug another piece of meat out of the cooler and threw more potatoes into the pot.

"Are you married?" asked Van Zyl.

Bertus and Elsie looked at each other and Elsie looked away into the night.

"No *Oom*," said Bertus, "only good friends."

"That's alright," said Van Zyl, "we do have two spare rooms."

Elsie was still looking into the night.

Van Zyl took them to a bathroom to get cleaned up and left them to get on with it.

They had both been given the chance to bath in a real bath before supper and Bertus felt very conscious of the way Elsie smelt when she sat next to him at table. The talk had been light. Bertus had told Van Zyl where they had come from but didn't say anything about the gold. He told them that they needed the wagon because they were looking to start farming in the Nelspruit area, as soon as they were married of course.

A good supper of meat, potatoes and vegetables and two mugs of coffee and they moved to the veranda. A middle-aged black woman came to fetch food presumably for her and her family. She greeted them pleasantly.

Bertus lay in a bed that smelt of soap, with his hands behind his head. He couldn't stop thinking of the way Elsie looked away when Van Zyl asked if they were married. It made him feel uneasy. He had always thought of Elsie as his friend. He tossed and turned and didn't have much of a good night's sleep. He thought about what he had said to Van Zyl about farming. He couldn't see himself going back to either one of their farms. He didn't really feel bitter toward the British but the farms held too many memories. It would be better if they started somewhere else and what Hannes had told him of Madagascar, it felt the natural thing to do. Hannes had told him that the French, who Madagascar seemed to belong to, were welcoming the Boers. They felt sorry for any man who had to live under British rule. It didn't occur to him that they would be living under French rule.

He flew out of bed with a cock crowing. They should have been long gone. They had breakfast but Bertus was jumpy and eager to get going. Elsie took the reins of a pair of strong cart mules. Bertus tied their horses behind and jumped up on the back of the cart. They said their good-byes and were about to leave when Van Zyl put his hand on the seat next to Bertus. "I saw some strange men pass the house early this morning," said Van Zyl, "they didn't look like a good bunch. This is my farm but they didn't have the decency to stop and greet me. They did see me. I think you must be very careful, be on the look-out." Bertus thanked him as they pulled away. He was almost sure that it was the bunch they had seen at the hotel in Nelspruit. He had had a bad feeling about them from the start.

"Keep your Mauser close," Bertus said to Elsie as she headed the mules up the incline into the foothills of the Drakensberg Mountains.

He didn't think it was too far to Rollo but they hadn't come this way before so he wasn't sure. The dirt road would take them there. He hadn't asked Van Zyl because he didn't want them to know exactly where they were going. Elsie kept the horses at a good pace. However far it was, Bertus was sure that they would get to the gold-site before dark. Bertus climbed into the back so that he was facing from where they had come. The mountains were beautiful and even the foothills made him doubt their decision to leave.

Mainly though, he faced to the rear to watch for the dust of anyone following them but he didn't see anything. At noon he took over the driving from Elsie after a short stop to rest the mules and let them drink from a crystal-clear stream coming down off the mountains. While they waited, Bertus made a small smokeless fire and boiled some water for coffee. They chewed on *biltong* and dried peaches while riding.

Bertus pulled the wagon to a halt on the river bank opposite the gold burial site as the sun was setting behind the mountains. It took all of Bertus' will power to leave the gold for the next morning. Elsie was so impatient that she struggled to keep her mind on the cooking. She didn't know exactly where the gold was buried and Bertus teased her by not telling. Finally, they pulled their blankets around themselves and tried to sleep. This high up in the mountains it tended to get cold at night even if it was hot in the daytime.

They heard the chuckle of hyenas further upstream, if you could call it upstream. The stream was down to a trickle and if it didn't rain good and hard soon, this river would dry up altogether. Of course, it would rain again and this river would rush and gurgle with the water climbing the banks. Bertus had a thought that it might even expose the gold, if they didn't get it out soon. Bertus and Elsie would only take a fair share, leaving the rest to be taken by the others. Hopefully they would dig it out before the river came down.

Bertus woke to hear the cough of a lion. He looked up at Orion's Belt and reckoned it to be about three in the morning. He had stood watch so many times on commando that he was quite accurate with telling time by the stars. The horses and mules were restless but Bertus put that down to the closeness of the hyenas and the lion. He walked over and spoke to the animals to calm them. The fire was very low so he threw a few logs on the flames and watched them flare up before pulling his blanket around himself. He wished that Hannes would catch up to them. He hated admitting it but he missed Hannes banter. He listened to Elsie breathing heavily in sleep and it had a calming effect on him, he was soon asleep again.

Bertus woke to drops of water on his face. It was still dark but close to dawn. The sky was dark and as he looked up a lightning bolt ripped the sky. Elsie came awake fast. It took Bertus a few seconds to remember the mine shaft. He jumped up, rolling his blanket as he walked to the wagon. They threw their saddles onto the wagon. The rain was falling faster now. "Come," shouted Bertus, thunder was rumbling, "there is a mine shaft where we can take shelter; up on the *kopje*."

Elsie jumped onto the cart beside him. Luckily it was already light enough to see the track and Bertus drove the mules, not too fast, up toward the mine shaft. Elsie pulled a tarpaulin over their backs and made noises to encourage Bertus. The mouth of the shaft was clear enough for them to drive straight in. "Be careful of snakes," shouted Elsie above the noise of the storm.

They sat for a minute on the wagon before climbing down and walking back to the mouth of the shaft. By this time, it was chucking it down and lightning was lacing the sky. They were both fairly wet despite their efforts to cover themselves. There was enough dry wood lying around to make a fire. Elsie pulled out her box of safety matches that she had carefully wrapped in greaseproof paper and the flames soon cheered them up. They stood, turning in front of the flames, laughing, trying to dry their clothes.

While Elsie broke eggs into a pan, Bertus walked into the shaft. He danced a few times when spider-webs grabbed his face. And he was very careful to watch out for snakes. He walked as far back as he could before it was too dark to see. Bertus found the gold bars that they had stacked behind a small rock-fall together with the bags of blank coins. He carried one bag with him when Elsie called down the tunnel for him to come and eat. He dropped the bag behind the wagon as he walked past. Right then he was more interested in food than in gold.

They ate watching the rain slowly subside. The rain had stopped completely by the time they went out to rinse their tin plates in a small stream that had formed just outside the shaft. Coffee tasted good and they stood around with their mugs full looking down into the valley. The shaft was positioned so that the river was out of site from the mouth of the shaft but they could hear the roar of water.

"Let's go look at the river," said Bertus as he tossed his mug onto the dry dust of the shaft floor.

The ground was slippery underfoot so they had to be careful going down. Coming around the side of the *kopje*, the sight that met their eyes was unbelievable. A few hours ago there was just a stream in the middle of the river-bed. Now there was a raging river stretching from one bank to the other. They helped each other over rocks until they were a few feet from the water.

They watched the water and debris swirling past. It was too noisy to talk but they stood for a while just watching. The gold burial site was deep underwater and Bertus worried if the water was going to wash the covering away. He motioned to Elsie for them to go back. As soon as they were far enough around the base of the *kopje* to hear each other speak, Bertus told Elsie about the gold under the river bed.

"We will have to wait for the water level to drop enough to see if the gold is exposed," said Bertus.

"That might take days," answered Elsie.

"I have to make sure for Hannes' sake," said Bertus, "if the gold is showing, it will be taken, for sure." He didn't want to say stolen because it was stolen in the first place.

They made their way back to the shaft and Bertus stoked the fire while Elsie went to find water for coffee. She didn't have to go far but took her rifle anyway. They sat on the tailgate of the wagon enjoying their coffee even though Bertus was worried.

"The worst that could happen is that we will have to do some covering again," said Elsie.

"But what if it rains again?" asked Bertus.

"Well we don't know yet if the river has exposed the gold," said Elsie.

"Where is your Mauser?" asked Bertus, looking around.

Elsie also looked around. She was sure that she had brought it back with her when she had gone to fetch water.

Bertus had forgotten the bag of coins that he had dropped beside the wagon. He was opening his mouth to tell Elsie about it and to suggest they take the mules and horses out when he froze. He pointed to the bag and she nodded but there were boot-prints in the dirt down the side of the wagon, on the side that he hadn't walked. Elsie was watching him. She could see something was wrong and he held up his hand for her to be quiet.

His Mauser was lying against a rock at the mouth of the shaft. Elsie slowly slipped off the wagon's tailgate and tried to look relaxed as she walked toward it. Bertus slowly stood and started walking toward the mouth of the shaft. As he touched his rifle, a man, one of those from the hotel, stepped into the mouth of the shaft, grinned and smashed him in the face with the butt of his rifle.

Elsie made a grab for Bertus' rifle but it was too late and she was miles too slow. A man stepped out from behind the wagon, grabbed the rifle with one hand and her wrist with the other.

"Hehehe," he giggled, "look what I have." He spoke Afrikaans.

Elsie screamed, looking toward Bertus, just in time to see him going down. The man who had hit Bertus, stepped over him with a wide grin on his face and walked to where Elsie was being held. Another man walked out from behind the wagon. All four of them were scruffy and dirty.

"Now look what you found, Kleinboet," said the one who had hit Bertus.

"You can have first go Ouboet," said the one holding Elsie, almost offering her to the one who had hit Bertus. He was still giggling.

Elsie relaxed slightly and then kneed him hard in the groin. He screamed and let go his grip on her wrist. Ouboet backhanded her viciously across the jaw and she fell unintentionally into the arms of one of the others. He laughed.

Kleinboet lunged forward, "I'll teach you," he shrieked.

The man holding her, swung her out of reach.

He laughed and hit Kleinboet in the mouth, "me first."

Ouboet started to say something but then thought better of it. He shrugged and turned away.

"As you like," he said, "pass her around, I'm not interested."

The others stood still for a few seconds.

"I'm next," shouted Kleinboet and got smacked in the mouth again.

He whimpered a bit but backed off.

Elsie saw that they kept on tripping over the bag of gold coins but didn't even look down. She realised then that they didn't know about the gold. She thought about bargaining, the gold for her virginity but knew that would only delay what was going to happen. They wouldn't keep to their side of any bargain. She began to sob.

Bertus stirred. He opened his eyes and got stomped with the rifle butt again for his trouble. He stayed conscious though and watched what was happening. "Don't take all day Tobias," Ouboet said to the man holding Elsie.

Tobias laughed and started dragging her behind the wagon. Again he tripped over the bag of gold without looking down. Granted the bag was only the size of a man's head and, made of greasy tarpaulin and covered with dust, it did look like a rock.

"Wait," called Bertus, "I know where gold is hidden." He tried not to whine.

Tobias carried on dragging Elsie. Kleinboet wasn't taking any notice. He was still giggling while following Tobias and Elsie.

"Stop!" shouted Ouboet.

Everyone froze. The others looked at him with puzzled expressions. Ouboet walked over to Bertus. "Where?" he shouted, raising the rifle again.

Bertus raised his arm in defence but shouted, "let her go and I will tell you."

Ouboet looked down at Bertus for a few seconds.

"Bertus, they will kill you after you give them the gold!" shouted Elsie.

"Shut -up!" shouted Tobias and lifted his arm to back-hand her again.

All the while the fourth man had been leaning against the wagon, now he stepped forward and bolted a round into the chamber of his rifle. It was a .303, more than likely taken off the body of a dead British soldier.

"Let him talk," he said, "all we have to lose is a bit of female fun that we can get anywhere."

"I agree with Jarius," said Ouboet. He turned to Tobias, "Let her go."

Kleinboet blubbered a bit but didn't say anything.

"They are going to kill you!" shouted Elsie again. This time Tobias did back-hand her and she stumbled to the mouth of the shaft.

Bertus didn't say anything. He knew he was a dead man but for the first time he knew deep inside that he had always loved Elsie. She stumbled out of the shaft as Ouboet and Jarius hauled Bertus to his feet.

"Alright, she is gone. Show us this gold that you were talking about," said Ouboet.

Bertus struggled to stay upright. He had fuzzy things in front of his eyes and the whole shaft was swaying. He wanted to give Elsie as much head-start as possible without driving these men to anger. The timing had to be right. He put his hand against the shaft wall to steady himself and slowly walked toward the wagon. He drew it out as long as possible but eventually he stood above the bag of gold.

"Get on with it!" shouted Tobias. He was actually standing over the bag himself.

Bertus pointed down to the bag. The men stared at him and then down at the bag. Bertus watched as it suddenly dawned on them what they were looking at. He watched as they slowly knelt, put their rifles to one side and leant forward to the bag, big mistake. Ouboet pulled it toward him, took out his knife and cut the *riem* binding the mouth of the bag. As the bag fell open, the gold coins spilt out into the dust.

Jarius must've realised that they had made a mistake. He grabbed for his rifle but Ouboet's rifle was already in Bertus' hands. As he brought it up, a flame boomed from the shaft entrance. Jarius and Tobias were thrown back against the wall of the shaft. Bertus worked another round into the chamber and threw a quick glace over his shoulder. Elsie was flying sideways into the shaft while working her bolt but Ouboet and Kleinboet weren't sitting idle.

If angels are sent

To do men's work,

Assist them

And speed them on their way.

Oupa Barron

CHAPTER 10

Unfortunately for Gideon Barron and his friends, the night of luxury had to come to an end. Gideon was very glad that they had slept in the house. Rain had thundered down for a while in the early hours of the morning. Gideon loved the sound of rain on a corrugated iron roof. He woke to the smell of eggs, bacon and steak cooking. Normally he would have woken before first light but he was able to switch off the alarm in his head when he didn't feel any urgency.

He had spent a lot of his waking hours lying on his bed trying to figure out what had happened to the gold. Firstly, who had taken it and why. Secondly, what plan did they have of getting rid of it and of course, where did they plan to get rid of it. Now he was eager to hear what the others thought.

By the time he arrived in the dining room, the others were already there with *Tannie* Betty fussing over them, ladling more eggs and bacon onto their plates. He saw her make a move to slide another piece of steak onto Lorraine's plate but Lorraine held up her hand so it went onto Johan's plate instead. When she saw Gideon walk into the room, she motioned him to a chair and started piling his plate.

Gideon sat down beside Lorraine and moved some sliced, fried tomato onto his steak before cutting an edge with a bit of fat and forking it into his mouth. *Tannie* Betty poured coffee from a big coffee pot into the mug in front of him. There was silence for a while, everyone chewing and drinking coffee, well not real silence, the chewing was a noise unto itself. Gideon watched them while he ate. They all knew how to eat properly with a knife and fork, a sure sign of good upbringing. Finally, they sat back, using the napkins to wipe their mouths.

While *Tannie* Betty was pouring coffee, she said with much pride in her voice, "the train came through this morning with a motor driven carriage on its way to Pietersburg. They call it a Motorcar."

"What?" asked Lorraine.

"I've heard of this," said Johan.

They all looked at each other but then went back to eating. It didn't seem to interest any of them.

"We have to think this through. We wasted so much time just blundering about the bush," said Gideon, getting back to their hunt for gold.

They all just looked at him, waiting for him to carry on. Johan grunted his agreement.

"We have to think, whoever took the gold must've had a plan. A plan of where to take it, how to get rid of it or who to sell it to."

"They could've taken it south, back to Jo'burg," suggested Johan.

Zandra clicked her tongue, "that would be foolish. If they were found by the Boers they would've been shot as traitors. Don't forget the war wasn't over yet, and if they were found by the Brits, they would've been shot anyway."

"If I was them, I would try to trade the gold for diamonds. Diamonds would be much easier to cart around," Lorraine offered. "The problem is where? Premier Diamond Mine is not far south from here. They could've arranged something with the officials." They all thought for a few seconds before all shaking their heads.

"There is only one sensible plan that they could've made," said Gideon.

"Yes," said Zandra, "east to the coast."

Gideon nodded. "If I were them, I would sell it piecemeal to pirates and ships captains and the only place that can handle ships big enough is Lorenco Marques."

"If they did that, wouldn't they have already sold it all off?" asked Lorraine.

"Well I, myself am not really interested in getting hold of the gold but merely clearing my name," said Gideon.

"It would be nice to get some of that gold," said Johan, "we have to set up new futures for ourselves." Everyone except Gideon nodded.

"Where can we get hold of a map?" asked Lorraine, "I am sure they would've taken the shortest route to Lorenco Marques."

"I think the shortest route is over the Crocodile River to Rossana Garcia and down to LM but we had better check on a map," said Johan.

They asked *Tannie* Betty and sure enough, she went and dug one out of some back room. She didn't want them to take it away but after a quick look they saw that Johan was right. The journey would take them past Elands River, then just north of Nelspruit, through a Drakensberg pass and on to Rossana Garcia. They would have to turn south at the mountains and cross the Crocodile River north of Nelspruit.

They finished off their breakfast with a few more cups of coffee and went to get their belongings from their rooms. Refreshed, it didn't take them long before they were heading along the road to Elands River. The road had shallow puddles of water and the air was fresh after the rain. By mid-morning they had reached the General Store at Elands River. The Indian owner greeted them like long lost family.

They only stayed long enough to buy some supplies before being on their way again. Johan passed a stick of *biltong* to each of them. Their spirits were riding high as they trotted down the road heading east. There were storm clouds in the east but Zandra assured them that they wouldn't get any rain that day. It took them two days to reach the foothills of the Drakensberg and this time the storm clouds looked ominous. They decided to overnight in the little town of Rolle.

They looked again for a local house that served supper and breakfast. This time it was a man and his wife, *Oom en Tannie* Van Rensburg. *Tannie Thia* was, once again, typical Boere wife, very friendly and fussing around making everyone comfortable.

The storm broke early, about mid-afternoon and the four of them stood in the lounge watching the rain hammer down in the street outside. First the big drops puffed in the dust but very soon the road was a river of water. Dogs ran for shelter and Lorraine spotted a cat drenched as it walked onto the veranda with a look on its face to make the dogs shy away.

As they watched, four British soldiers pulled their horse into the stables across the street. The four watched them dismount and after handing their horses to the stable-hand, walked back inside to where Gideon's little party had, a little earlier, brushed and fed their horses. They then turned to face the house where Gideon and his friends were standing. They couldn't be seen of course because of a lace curtain in the window

"What now?" asked Johan, looking at Gideon.

They had left their rifles in their rooms and Gideon felt naked without his Mauser in his hands.

"The war is over," said Zandra but she didn't sound very convinced.

"Should we run for it?" asked Johan, still looking at Gideon.

"Our horses are in the stable," Lorraine pointed out.

By this time the soldiers were walking across the street.

Suddenly *Tannie Thia* came into the room behind them.

"Don't worry, don't worry," she said, "the war is over. They may be looking for deserters."

Gideon didn't relax. He had a knot in his stomach. These men looked determined. They stopped on the front veranda to take off their coats, shaking the water from them but then leaving them outside. They came through the front door, making quite a noise with their boots on the wooden floor. They were dressed in khaki uniforms with khaki helmets which they immediately took off and held under their left arms. The right arm was ready for action.

Tannie Thia hustled out to them in the entrance passage.

"Gentlemen, how can I help you? Do you need rooms for the night?" she spoke Afrikaans.

"Good afternoon ma'am," said the officer in English. From where he stood, Gideon thought he was wearing three stars of a captain.

"Only something to eat ma'am but first we would like to speak to the riders of those four horses in the stables."

"I don't know who they belong to," said *Tannie Thia*. She spoke English now.

Gideon's gut told him to run for the rifles and he could see that the other three were turning on their toes, to move.

He stepped forward into the passage, "Good afternoon," he said in English.

All the soldiers turned to face him. They all carried pistols in holsters and their right hands settled gently on the holster covers. These aren't ordinary soldiers, Gideon thought to himself.

"Good afternoon sir," said the officer, "may we speak with you and your party?" he asked politely.

Gideon was wound like a string on a guitar but he stepped to one side and gestured for the soldiers to move into the lounge. The last one in was a youngster with blond hair and Gideon followed him into the lounge. Lorraine, Zandra and Johan looked like spring-hares caught in the lamplight of an open kitchen door. When they were all in, the officer turned to face Gideon but as he spoke, he twisted his body to include them all.

"I assume you men have handed in your rifles to the local garrison?" he asked.

They all nodded, not looking at each other.

"Good, well all that is left for you to do is sign the Treaty of Vereeniging, a copy of which I have here," he added, "unless you have already signed?"

Gideon and Johan shook their heads.

"What is it?" asked Gideon.

"It is the treaty that your leaders have already signed in Vereeniging. Shortly you are signing to say you submit yourselves to British rule. Gentlemen," he added as both Gideon and Johan started shuffling, "the alternative left to you is that you leave the country. If you somehow leave here today without signing, you will be given a month to pack and leave, after which you will be branded as criminals and hunted down as such."

"May we have a few minutes to discuss this amongst ourselves?" asked Gideon.

"Of course," said the officer, who turned out to be a captain as Gideon had guessed. "We will be staying for dinner, so should we meet in the dining room after we have eaten?"

"Yes," agreed Gideon.

The captain nodded and the soldiers walked to a table with four chars and sat down. Gideon gestured to the others to follow him and led them to his bedroom.

"It seems that women don't have to sign this so-called treaty," said Zandra, sounding a bit indignant.

"Ag don't be disappointed," said Johan, "you are lucky." He turned to Gideon, "so what are we going to do?"

"You must make your own mind up," answered Gideon, "but I don't want to leave my country so I will sign, all our leaders have anyway."

Johan sat down on the bed and stared at the wall, "but under British rule?" he said eventually.

"What difference is it going to make," said Zandra. "We never hear from the government on our farms anyway. Even the Boer government didn't come and help us when we were attacked by the Xhosas."

They sat awhile deep in thought.

"What do you think?" Gideon asked Lorraine softly.
"I don't see that you have any option, if you want to live in peace in your country."
"It won't be our country anymore," said Johan bitterly.
They sat quietly again for a while.
"Let's go eat," suggested Gideon, "I am going to sign."

After hiding their rifles in the bushes outside the house, they met again in the lounge and trooped into the dining-room to eat. The soldiers were already seated and the Captain nodded to them.
After a few helpings of lamb stew with thick slices of homemade bread and farm butter, washed down with a couple of cups of coffee, they started feeling better and the world looked brighter.

The three other soldiers stayed seated while the Captain moved to a cleared table in the corner of the dining room. The copy of the treaty was set out with a dip-pen, ink-well and blotter. Gideon signed first with a very reluctant Johan sitting down after him. They both signed two copies, one each to take away with them. The Captain stood up and shook their hands. He rolled up the signed copies and carefully put them in a leather holder.

"Thank you, gentlemen," he said seriously, "we will now be taking your leave."

The other soldiers followed him out the door and they soon heard the horse's hooves as they rode away.

It took some time and a few brandies to console Johan but eventually they managed to get him to take his copy of the treaty and helped him stagger off to bed. Zandra carefully put the document in his saddle-bag. They went back to the lounge and sipped brandy until the clock on the wall showed ten o' clock and the waiter came to tell them that the bar was now closed. They watched the local men troop out of the bar. Of course, women weren't allowed in a men's bar. Even so, they sat a bit longer. Talking about living under the English and Gideon reminding them every now and again that it was the British, not just the English.

They collected their rifles from outside, the soldiers hadn't mentioned the rifles but it was good to be sure. The girls were sharing a room, by choice. Gideon waited in his room for them to tell him they were finished in the bathroom. He soaked until his bathwater started cooling, not knowing when he would get a chance again. He lay in the bath and fingered his scars, thinking of the way "Reintjies" had saved his life.

They wanted to leave early and thought they were going to have to miss breakfast but *Tannie Thea* had *mieliemeel* porridge with pumpkin fritters ready for them and, of course, cups of coffee.

The soldiers had ridden west the night before; they were riding east, into the sunrise so hopefully they wouldn't meet up again soon. The road was wet from the rain the previous evening. Gideon thought about the soldiers sleeping out in the wet. Maybe there was a regimental camp near-by with big tents and raised beds. There were enough times when Gideon slept out in the rain during the war.

As they approached the foothills of the Drakensberg, the streams they crossed were swollen from the rain. One of them that they had to cross had broken its banks so they couldn't see where the actual river bank was. They sat their horses looking at it, trying to make up their minds what to do. Gideon rode upstream a way and Johan road downstream, looking for a safe place to cross. They weren't worried about crocs in this swirling mass. Crocodiles weren't stupid, they would stay on the bank until this went down.

Gideon and Johan met again with the girls.
"I found a place," said Johan speaking loud enough above the noise of the river to be heard. "Not the ideal place but at least you can see the bank so we will know where it drops away."
"I've got nothing," said Gideon.
"Not much choice then," said Zandra.
Johan pulled his horse around and one by one they followed him. He stopped at the place he thought was safest and waited for them.

"Once you are in and you feel your horse swimming, don't try to beat the current." Said Gideon. "Swim with the current, slowly making your way across."

"I'll go first," said Johan.

"Ok and I'll go last," said Gideon.

They looked at each other, silently wishing each other good luck and Johan let his horse feel it's way into the water. Zandra went next, followed by Lorraine. Gideon watched them for a minute before urging his horse forward. He glanced at Johan in front, he was off the side of his horse holding the saddle and swimming nicely, letting the current take him and slowly pushing toward the other bank.

Gideon followed Loraine but he too slid off the saddle as soon as his horse was swimming. He could feel the currents swirling below him. His feet didn't touch the ground. His horse seemed to sense that he should swim diagonally toward the opposite bank. Things were going well but then he saw Zandra seem to wobble on the saddle. Johan, who was closest to her shouted for her to slide off but whether she heard or not Gideon couldn't tell. She seemed to lose her balance and went in head first.

She came up about six foot from her horse, kicking and spluttering. She tried to strike out to grab her saddle but her horse spooked and shied away.

"Just relax!" screamed Johan, "leave the horse! Make your way to the bank!"

She heard him now and did as he said. Meanwhile Lorraine realised that it was best swimming next to her horse and was doing well. Zandra reached the opposite bank just after her horse and after a few attempts slipping and falling, managed to pull herself out. Her horse waited patiently for her

Johan was out next and after slipping and sliding made his way back to where Zandra was on her knees in the mud. Johan helped her to her feet. Lorraine floated quite a way downstream but managed to get out with her horse without much trouble. Gideon let his horse float down after Lorraine. The bank there was firmer and his horse hauled him out. The others slowly made their way down the edge of the bank toward Gideon. They were all soaking wet and covered in mud. They all looked to their rifles but they had all strapped their rifles to their saddles and so were fine.

Nobody said anything, they just grunted and nodded to each other. They led their horses a little way from the river. It was quieter so they could talk without screaming at each other. They wiped their horses down and checked that they hadn't lost anything while battling the water. Next, they cleaned their rifles.

"Let's find a place where we can change," said Zandra trying to wipe her face but only succeeding in smearing it and making it worse, "we will have to just roll up our muddy clothes until we can find some cleanish water to wash ourselves and our clothes." Johan smiled at her but didn't say anything.

They walked their horses along a path, up, through the bush toward a *kopje*. Again, Johan led the way with Gideon coming up in the rear. Gideon wasn't really concentrating; he was replaying the river crossing in his mind. That had been dangerous and could have ended badly.

They all stopped suddenly in their tracks as a burst of gunfire burst out from a way, quite close, in front of them. They all stood listening. It carried on for a few minutes, sharp bursts, a number of rifles and maybe a Webly in play. Some of the shots sounded hollow. They moved cautiously now and came into a small clearing in front of an old mine shaft. The shooting had stopped but they still moved cautiously forward. A wagon was backing out the shaft pushed by two mules walking backward. Nobody was holding the mules and they looked nervous. Johan grabbed the reins and stroked them, talking to them to calm them down.
They tied their horses to some bushes and, holding their rifles at the ready, moved slowly into the mouth of the shaft.

War does not determine who is right

Only who is left

Bertrand Arthur William Russell

CHAPTER 11

There seemed to be bodies everywhere. Johan knelt at the first body just inside the entrance.

"It's a woman," he said, "and she's alive," he was feeling her neck, "but only just, three bullets," he said by way of explanation.

Zandra went to her and the others moved on into the shaft. A man was moaning deeper in the darkness. Gideon left the other bodies and went straight to the one that was obviously alive. It was a young man in his late teens. He was bleeding badly. Gideon ripped his own shirt of even though it was wet and muddy. He tore the youngster's shirt off and saw that there were two holes in the lower abdomen. He balled his shirt and held it against the wounds but the shirt was almost immediately soaked.

"Ok boy," he said, "soon the pain will be gone."

Gideon knew that it would be only a matter of
minutes before he would be dead.

"Have you got a message for anyone,"

"Hehehe," the youngster giggled as his head fell to
the side.

Gideon looked around. He noticed gold coins strewn
across the floor of the shaft but he was more
interested in the other bodies. He checked the other
three in turn but couldn't get a pulse on any of them.
Two had long beards and he took his time making
sure under the beards that there was no pulse. He
went back to where the girls were working on the
wounded young woman. He was shooed away.

"You and Johan go and find honey," said Lorraine, "I
need to dress her wounds as I did yours. She is
unconscious so we are going to take advantage of that
to get the bullets out."

Gideon and Johan moved to the entrance of the shaft.
Suddenly Johan knelt in the sand.

"Blood," he said sticking his finger in a black patch.

They looked ahead and could clearly see the trail of black patches. With rifles at the ready again, they followed the trail. It led up the side of the *kopje.* The ground had dried enough for the trail to be clear. They didn't have far to go. They saw a man sitting on a boulder, looking down at the river. Gideon looked into the valley but couldn't see anything of interest. He did see a honey badger but it was ambling along on the other side river bank. The man wasn't carrying a rifle and was hatless. He had dark hair and beard. The back of his shirt was a mixture of red and black. The red glistened, fresh blood. He didn't turn as Johan and Gideon moved up to him, well spread out just in case.

As Gideon reached him, he opened his mouth to speak but blood dribbled over his bottom lip. He tried again, "the name is Jarius," he managed. "Are they all dead?" he asked.

"Yes," answered Gideon.

"I didn't shoot anyone," Jarius carried on, "just in the wrong place at the wrong time."

He swayed and Johan caught him from the other side. They knew that if he lay down, he would drown in his own blood.

"What happened?" asked Gideon softly.

"I was on my way home," he gurgled a bit, "no more home. My wife and daughter died in the *khaki's* concentration camp."

"What happened in the mine shaft?" Gideon asked again.

"They thought they could have gold," Jarius said. Gideon remembered the gold coins.

"But they thought they could also have the girl," Jarius was going limp fast.

Gideon and Johan tried to hold him up but he was going too fast. He spat blood and closed his eyes. The next words were just bubbles of bright red blood. He slipped off the boulder and they lowered him gently to the ground.

"First we need the honey comb," said Johan looking down toward the river, trying to pick up where they had seen the honey badger.

Gideon didn't fancy fording that river again even though the level had dropped significantly. Johan pointed. The badger was now on their side. The bees must have led him to cross.

They made their way down the river bank. Quickly rinsing the blood off their hands, they followed in the direction of the badger. Johan pointed out the bird that was leading the badger to the bee-hive.

The honey was in a hollow tree that was overhanging the river. Gideon was going to light a handful of grass to smoke the hive but before he had the chance, Johan stuck his arm into the hive and brought out a good size slab of honeycomb. They quickly moved away from the hive and made their way back to the shaft.

They looked in on the girls and told them about Jarius.

"We still don't know what happened," said Johan.

The girls both shook their heads.

Their patient started regaining consciousness, groaning. Lorraine moved the shirt that was covering her so the boys moved away.

She started mumbling so they moved closer again.

"Bertus?" she was asking, "is Bertus alive?"

Lorraine sadly shook her head.

The girl became very agitated, "no, no," she said, "he must be alive, the blond one."

Lorraine nodded to Gideon, "look again."

Half reluctantly, Gideon went from body to body. It was hard to distinguish the hair colour with the dust and blood. One body was propped against the wall and with a closer examination he saw that he had blond hair, and he found a very faint pulse. Gideon called Johan over and together they carefully opened and removed his blood caked shirt. They carefully wiped the blood away with the shirt. He had two holes high on his chest above the heart only a thumb length away from each other, very accurate shooting but a little high, rifle shots for sure. Lifting him away from the wall, they saw that the bullets had gone right through. There was only a trickle coming from the wounds but the bullets had made a mess of the flesh around the holes.

Lorraine came over and started fussing over him. She had her spare pair of trousers that she had fetched from her saddle bag and bandaged a large piece of honeycomb over both wounds. She dribbled water from her water-bottle into his mouth. Gideon felt again for a pulse, it was very slightly stronger.

Zandra had Johan build a fire just inside the entrance and she boiled some leaves in their coffee pot. Now how are we going to make coffee, thought Johan but he knew he dare not say anything.
Neither of their two patients had any blood in the mouth so Lorraine got the men to lay them down. Gideon formed the sand under them so that the torso was slightly higher. The man, whom they assumed was Bertus, was very pale and hadn't regained consciousness. The girl had also lost consciousness so didn't know that Bertus was still alive. Loraine had removed the bullets while the girl was unconscious and was positive that at least this one would survive.

The men carried the two dead bodies out to where Jarius was lying. They covered the bodies with rocks to keep the carrion from getting to them. They had searched the bodies for any letters or photo's that would give them an indication of who the men were but there was nothing.

That night the four friends sat around the fire cooking meat and *mielies*. The *mielies* they left in their husks and pushed them under the coals to bake. Zandra produced another coffee pot so Johan felt better.

"What in the world happened here?" asked Lorraine of no one in particular.

They spoke about it until Orion's Belt was on its way down but couldn't make sense of it.

"There must be a connection between Bertus and the girl," said Zandra, "but whether boyfriend or brother we don't know."

"Ja, no rings," added Johan, "but we can ask her when she comes 'round."

"Jarius mentioned gold," said Gideon, "I suppose it's the gold coins we picked up out of the dirt. I didn't see any gold coin when we were loading at Pienaar's River"

They nodded.

"Must be worth quite a bit," said Johan.

"We don't know who it belongs to," added Gideon, "they could've been fighting over it."

"Let's wait for the girl to come 'round," said Lorraine.

They sat in silence for a while longer.

Gideon stood up, "I'll take first watch on our patients."

They nodded and he walked away to position himself between the girl and Bertus. He thought about them for a while but then pushed the thoughts to one side. It was no use making stories in his head. He turned his thoughts to Lorraine. How was he going to persuade her that he hadn't been part of the robbery of the gold bullion. Every avenue had, so far, led to nothing. He owed Lorraine his life and even if they parted at the end of this, it was important for him that she believe him.

He almost dozed off but he caught movement out the corner of his eye. His hand went to his rifle but then he saw that it was Bertus. He was trying to pull himself up. Gideon quickly moved over to him and helped him to turn slightly. The floor must be hard for someone hurt as badly as this. Bertus had his eyes open.

"Elsie?" he said the name as a question.

Gideon assumed that must be the girl, "alive," he stated.

Bertus closed his eyes again and seemed to be breathing easier. Well at least they knew their names now. Gideon tried to make Bertus more comfortable and then moved to Elsie to check on her. Her breathing seemed regular so he sat down where he had been before. It seemed no time at all before Lorraine came out of the darkness to relieve him. He told her that Bertus had regained consciousness long enough to ask about Elsie. Apart from that, they didn't speak but Gideon was very aware of Lorraine's body heat and smell.

He walked to the fire. Johan was sitting there sucking on his pipe. The tobacco smell was quite pleasant. They sat in silence watching the small flames dance. Gideon poured two cups of coffee.

"So, what are your plans after this?" asked Johan.

Gideon shrugged, "and you?" he asked.

"I've spoken to Zandra," said Johan a bit sheepishly, "maybe we will hook up. If her father and brothers come back from the war, we will move to my farm. We would get married first of course," he added hastily. He looked across at Gideon, "and you, what about you and Lorraine?"

Gideon scratched with a stick in the dirt, "I don't think Lorraine will have me until I can prove that I wasn't part of the robbery of Kruger's gold."

"I think she believes you already," answered Johan.

Gideon didn't say anything. They sat there sipping their coffee. The river had dropped enough so that there was no roaring sound in the valley anymore. Johan got up to relieve Lorraine. Time had gone by very quickly, thought Gideon. He lay down near to the fire and allowed himself to doze. He half heard Lorraine moving about, maybe pouring coffee and felt strangely comfortable. His shoulder still ached occasionally but he could live with that. He felt someone shaking him awake.

"The girl is awake," said Zandra.

Gideon rolled onto his knees and up and followed Zandra to where Lorraine and Johan were on their haunches beside Elsie.

"She says that she and Bertus are friends," whispered Lorraine, "and that all the other men attacked them." Elsie started speaking then and told them bits and pieces of what had happened. The trouble was she kept on slipping in and out of consciousness.

"I think we know enough to let her sleep now," said Lorraine giving Elsie a sip of water.

They still only had bits and pieces but now they knew that Elsie and Bertus had been in the shaft, sheltering from the storm when the four other men had attacked them. According to Elsie it wasn't to rob them because they hadn't known about the bag of gold. It was for the sole purpose of raping Elsie. Bertus had promised the men gold if they would allow Elsie to leave but when they had agreed, Elsie hadn't believed them and was sure that they would kill Bertus to leave no witnesses. So she had come back in time for the gun battle.

At daylight the men started saddling up but Lorraine stopped them, "they won't be able to be moved until they are stronger, especially Bertus."

When she saw Gideon's disappointment she added, "maybe tomorrow or the next day."

The level of the river continued dropping during that day and by the next morning it was down to a narrow river in the middle of a wide bed. By this time Bertus was fully conscious and corroborated Elsie's story. Bertus' wound seemed to heal faster than Elsie's, maybe because the shots had gone clean through and not done any major damage.

Johan and Gideon tried to explore deeper into the mine shaft but after coming across a nest of puff-adders, they decided not to go beyond the daylight line. Anyway, they were kept busy hunting for the pot and collecting herbs that the women needed for the wounds and medicinal soup.

That night they sat around the fire discussing the situation.

"We must first take these two back to Nelspruit to a hospital," said Lorraine.

"Yes," agreed Johan, "we can't take them with us and we can't leave them here."

"How far are we going to go, looking for the stolen gold?" asked Zandra.

"Well I only want to clear my name," answered Gideon.

"But that may take us in to Mozambique," said Zandra with some frustration in her voice.

Gideon shrugged. They were quiet after that. The jackals were starting to howl and the guinee-fowl were making a racket finding a roost out of reach of the predators but Gideon picked up another sound coming from inside the shaft. He stood up, scooping his rifle on the way up.

It was Bertus trying to draw their attention so he went over and knelt beside him. He wasn't there long before he came back to the fire.

"Bertus says he has something to tell us," he said, "but he wants us all there to tell us. "together.""

They gathered around Bertus. He still looked weak but he was fully conscious.

"Bertus," Elsie's voice came from the darkness.

"Don't worry," he called to her, "I know what I must say."

They were curious now.

"I heard you speaking earlier about the stolen gold," he started. "I know who stole the gold from the Boers."

Well they were all ears now and moved closer.

"Bring him some water," said Lorraine.

They waited for Johan to get back with the water.

"Part of the commando that I was with at Pienaar's River planned to steal it, I heard them planning the robbery. I tried to warn the *Veldkornet* but I was too late. I followed them to Elands River and picked up Elsie on the way."

"Ja," said Elsie in the dark, "we followed them but the river held us up."

"Ja," agreed Bertus, "someone must have left this one bag of gold coins here but they surely took all the gold bullion with them to Lorenco Marques."

"Ja," said Elsie, "they must be on a ship by now."

"Who was it?" asked Johan venomously, "was it these four that you killed."

Bertus winced at the thought that they had killed four men, "no," he said, "these came later."

"We only heard first names," said Elsie, "we heard the names Pieter and Jakes, that's all."

"Think hard," said Gideon urgently, "did you hear anything else?"

"No," said Elsie and Bertus shook his head.

Bertus lay back exhausted after the stress of telling his tale.

"Ok, relax now," said Lorraine as she stood up, "it doesn't matter anymore. They have gone and the gold has gone with them."

"I think we must get you to the hospital in Nelspruit," said Zandra also standing up. "We should leave tomorrow morning," she said turning to Gideon.

"Is there a hospital in Nelspruit?" asked Gideon.

"I don't know," answered Zandra, "but they need better care than we can give them."

That evening, while the girls made supper, Johan and Gideon made ready for the next day. They made a bed on the wagon and gently lifted Elsie and Bertus up onto the wagon. They would still have to span in the mules and saddle the horses in the morning. The horses belonging to the four horsemen and the two belonging to Elsie and Bertus, they tied behind the wagon. Johan was going to drive the wagon so his horse went behind the wagon too.

Lorraine fed the two in the wagon before joining the other three at the fire.

As always, the supper was a grand affair washed down with lots of coffee. Johan lit his pipe and they sat back to talk about their situation. A baboon troop had moved into the *kloof* above the river and the four listened to the bark of the troop leader calling them all to safety. The jackals wouldn't go near them but a leopard might try to steal a young one during the night. Leopards enjoyed a bit of young baboon meat.

"What are we going to do once we have loaded these two off?" asked Johan.

Gideon looked across at Lorraine, "do you believe me now?" he asked her.

"Does it matter?" she asked.

"Yes," he said, "it is important to me."

"Ja," she sighed, as if it was a big effort. She was quiet for a few seconds, then, "what do you plan to do after this?"

Gideon was quiet and Johan and Zandra made as if they weren't there.

"Would you join me on my farm?" he asked self-consciously.

"I will see if my father and brothers have come back from the war," she sounded a bit tense.

Gideon wondered if he had said something wrong, "alright, we can talk about it."

When with the abundance of things we posses
We have lost our thirst for the waters of life
Having fallen in love with life
We have ceased to dream of eternity
Sir Francis Drake; 1577

CHAPTER 12

They crossed the river at daybreak. It wasn't much of a river now. Bertus pulled himself up in the wagon to look along the riverbed but all looked covered for the time being. Elsie looked at him questioningly. He smiled and shook his head before lying back again.

The journey was very bumpy for Elsie and Bertus coming down out of the mountains but once they were in the rolling hills, the track became smoother. It became obvious that they weren't going to reach Nelspruit by the end of the day. The road or track curved down next to the Crocodile River. Gideon knew that Nelspruit was built on the banks of the river so he knew they were moving in the right direction. They had curved down from the north to join the road between Nelspruit and the coast.

There were plenty of places to make camp but they had to make sure that they weren't too close to the river where hippos would be a danger. Even collecting water to drink and cook was dangerous. They knew that they were not far from Nelspruit but it would've been madness to carry on in the dark. Anyway, another night wouldn't make much difference to Elsie and Kobus.

They had enjoyed their meal and were drinking coffee when a call came from the darkness, "*aandag die kamp*!"

Gideon and Johan stood up holding their rifles at the ready.

"*Kom in*!" called Johan.

A man walked into the firelight out of the darkness, leading his horse. He tied his horse to a tree just on the edge of the light.

"Good evening," he said in Afrikaans, lifting his hat. He was wearing a dark coloured suit with a black hat and dark brown boots. At first he looked well-dressed but as he came further into the light, they could see that the suit was shabby although clean. He had a full beard but not long and was carrying a Mauser rifle in his left hand. He had a guinea-fowl feather in his hat band.

"Brand," he said by way of introducing himself. He was a heavily built man.

Gideon nodded, "please join us," he indicated with his rifle to a place next to the fire.

"Thank you," Brand acknowledged. "I would appreciate a cup of coffee."

Zandra almost jumped forward to pour a cup for him. They let him settle back and relax before looking at him expectantly.

"We have been trying to get the farms back that the Pedi settled on during the war," he cupped his hands around his mug. "The British commander, Redvers Buller, supplied them with arms to take over the farms in this area from the women left on the farms while their men were away."

"I thought it was the Ndzundza who were living in this area?" asked Zandra, "they were living alongside the Boers."

"Yes, they were," answered Brand, "but the British promised them the farms and supplied them with guns so they turned against us. It was Matsitsi who turned his people against us after he was promised the earth."

"Are you winning?" asked Johan.

"In the end we will win," said Brand positively, "most of the Pedi are not born to stay in one place. Our big problem is that a lot of the farms have just been abandoned. Either the owners are dead or they have left the area or even the country."

They sat and digested this news for a while before Brand became curious.

"It is none of my business," he said, "but if you would like to tell me what you are doing here?" Gideon noticed that he had shifted his position so that his Mauser was in an easier angle.

"Relax," said Gideon and he explained that they were taking two wounded to Nelspruit. He called to Bertus to confirm what he had just said.

Bertus waved his arm above the side of the wagon, "ja, ja!" he called.

Brand physically relaxed and nodded. He went back to sipping his coffee. Zandra stood and poured them all more coffee.

"If you don't mind, I will make camp just a little way away? We will be safer in each other's company," asked Brand.

Gideon shrugged and looked around at the others. They all nodded.

"Thank you," said Brand standing up and handing the mug back to Zandra.

He walked to his horse and led him away into the bush a way beyond the light.

Gideon waited for him to get beyond hearing distance before he said, "do you believe him?"

"I believe him but that doesn't mean I trust him," said Johan softly.

"Why?" asked Zandra

"Just a feeling" answered Johan, "I was very conscious of the bag of gold coins at Elsie's feet."

"Well we should keep a watch anyway," said Gideon.

Johan took first watch, Gideon taking the middle watch. He kept a good eye on Brand's camp but nothing stirred. The jackals kept up their howling and all the usual night sounds that Gideon knew and loved. When Orion's belt was three quarters of the way across the sky, he woke Zandra.

"Anything?" she asked.

"No," said Gideon as he pulled his blanket around him.

At dawn Zandra woke them. Brand was gone.

"He left a short while ago, just as the birds started their noise," said Zandra.

The water was already boiling for coffee.

Before they moved off, Bertus called to them, "Elsie and I want to share the gold with you."

They came to the edge of the wagon.

"We feel that, because you saved our lives, we want to share the coins equally with you all."

"I don't really want anything," said Gideon, "I was accused of stealing it at one stage."

"Don't be silly," said Lorraine, "gold will help us to get started again."

"You don't have to do this," protested Zandra.

Gideon stayed quiet after that. None of the others argued against the idea.

They waited for Bertus to count out the coins and each of them found a bag to put their share in.

It didn't take them long to reach Nelspruit. They never saw any sign of Brand.

The wagon rolled down the main street. There wasn't a hospital in sight but in the middle of town they came across the Fig Tree Hotel with a big 1891 above the main entrance. Gideon swung down and went in. He was met in the entrance by the inevitable middle-aged woman who greeted him.

There was no hospital in town but a doctor had moved in to town just at the end of the war and had set up his rooms in a house on the western side of town. Gideon promised to be back and went out to give the news to the others.

The doctor's house was easy to find. It had a brass plate on one of the pillars of the veranda.

A black woman came to the door when he knocked and, opening the screen door, motioned him into the lounge. He heard her talking to someone further back in the house and soon a man followed her out. He was shorter than Gideon, clean shaven. He didn't look much older than Gideon but he had pure white hair brushed back on his head. He was wearing braces holding up his trousers and Gideon could see highly polished brown shoes peeping out from under the black trouser turn-ups.

"Can I help?" he asked in Afrikaans.

"Yes please," answered Gideon and gave him a short version of the story.

"Bring them in, bring them in," he said, already with a worried look on his face.

The black woman helped them get the two patients into two separate rooms. There were only the bags that the girls had found on the horses and the gold coins hidden in those bags. After saying goodbye

there wasn't much else to do but leave Elsie and
Bertus in the care of the doctor. It seemed that they
were already on the mend and they had the means to
pay for their care.

"We'll stable your mules and horses and leave your
wagon in the doctor's backyard." Zandra assured
them.

The four walked back to the hotel and booked in. In
the entrance of the hotel there were some photographs
and a printed account of the history of the Nel
brothers who had settled there years ago, grazing their
cattle there and attracting settlers to the area, some for
farming and some prospecting for gold.

They took four rooms and carried their bags in after
seeing to the horses. They decided to take the four
loose horses from the robbers, home with them.

Gideon lay soaking in the bath. He had shaved. Hair
on the face irritated him. Most of his thoughts centred
around Lorraine. He would have to work harder at
this although she had made it clear that they were
riding back together. She had told him to accept the

gold from Elsie and Bertus and had said they would need it.

He came out of his daydreaming with a banging on the bathroom door.

"You are not the only guest in the hotel!" it was Zandra.

It was dark by the time they had finished supper and met on the veranda. The aroma of Johan's tobacco hung in the air.

"I don't think those two were completely truthful with us," he said around the mouthpiece of his pipe.

That quickly attracted their attention and they all seemed to pull themselves forward.

"What do you mean?" asked Gideon.

"I had the feeling that there was more to the gold than they told us."

"Well we were in that shaft for four days in total and I didn't see any more gold," said Gideon.

The girls nodded in agreement.

"We never went into the back of the cave," said Johan.

"It wasn't safe," protested Zandra, "it looked as if it was going to cave in."

"And there were snakes in there," added Lorraine.

"What better place to hide your gold," said Johan.

They were quiet for a while, each digesting this information.

"I have a good mind to go back there," Johan added.

"I really don't want to," said Lorraine with apprehension in her voice.

"Neither do I," said Zandra, "we have enough gold and we have a farm to go back to. Please Johan," she finally pleaded.

"I am definitely not going back," retorted Gideon, "I didn't want any of the gold to start with. I would rather give you my share than see you go back."

Lorraine nodded.

"That gold could make us all rich," said Johan with a new sparkle in his voice.

"Please no," pleaded Zandra again.

They sat quietly but Johan was puffing on his pipe now.

"I am going back," he finally announced, "I will leave in the morning."

"Can't we talk you out of it?" asked Gideon.

Zandra groaned and sat for a while, "I will go with you," she said softly.

Johan smiled and sat back. Then he leant forward and squeezed Zandra's hand.

The evening ended in gloom for everyone except Johan. He became more excited as the evening wore on. He tried to persuade Gideon but there was no way Gideon wanted anything more to do with this gold that had caused him so much trouble, blood, sweat and tears.

The girls hugged each other. They had been through a lot together.

"Good luck, and I really mean it," said Gideon shaking Johan's hand.

Zandra hugged Gideon. She had tears in her eyes.

"Why so much gloom?" asked Johan.

Nobody added to what had already been said.

Early the next morning Johan went looking for another wagon and mules. He didn't want to ask Bertus because that would give a clue of what he was about to do. He also went looking for dynamite.

"What for," asked Zandra.

"Just in case there is rock that we need to move," Johan answered.

"Do you at least know how to use the stuff," Zandra protested.

"I used it during the war."

He found a general store that stocked explosives. He told the proprietor that he needed to move some rock on his farm. He also bought fuses that had the detonator already crimped onto the fuse and a copper spike to make a hole in the explosive sticks. The owner threw two lighting sticks into the box. The dynamite was immersed in axel-grease in a red wooden box.

Johan knew how to charge a stick of dynamite; he had done it many times blowing up railway lines and bridges. He knew that even a copper spike had to be pressed slowly into the dynamite. He had heard of men using a six-inch nail but he had heard of men blowing themselves up too.

Zandra met him at the hotel and tied their horses to the back of the wagon. Gideon and Lorraine walked onto the veranda and waved good-bye to them. They both thought that Johan was doing a foolish thing. They had more gold than they would ever need. Once Johan and Zandra had left, Gideon and Lorraine left for the Northern Transvaal and the Springbok Flats.

Johan and Zandra took things easy. Johan knew that they wouldn't reach the shaft before nightfall. It was close to midday by the time they left Nelspruit. They camped in the same spot that they had when they had met Brand. They watched out for him but they never saw him. There was a strange feel about the camp site and they nearly moved on but, in the end, stayed the night.

From there they cut north toward Rolle. Storm clouds were on the horizon when they started out the next morning, making them apprehensive. If that river came down in flood again, they would have to wait it out. They couldn't cross with the wagon if it was even close to being as full as it was before, when the four of them had crossed. Luckily the storm never broke.

It was late afternoon when they crossed the river bed and climbed the incline up to the shaft. If they hadn't known where it was, they would've missed it. They tethered the mules, wagon and horses outside the shaft, near to where they had covered the dead bodies with rocks. It seemed, to Zandra, such a long time ago. The mules and horses seemed to sense the dead bodies even though there was no smell. Claw marks could be seen where predators had tried to get to the bodies.

Johan and Zandra shared the watch during the night but Zandra was restless throughout the night. Even the horses were restless. The heavens opened up that night. They were very glad that they were well sheltered in the shaft. Johan brought the mules and horses into the entrance. They built up the fire and lit the storm lantern to try to make the place a bit cheerful.

The storm broke toward morning. By daybreak, the river was again rising.

"If we don't leave now, we are going to be stuck here for a couple of days," said Zandraconcerned.

"What does it matter," answered Johan, it wasn't a question, "we can spend that time searching for the gold."

Zandra was quiet. She knew that she had fallen in love with Johan but this gold fever was changing him. It rained most of the day but they worked toward the back of the shaft where they hadn't been before so they didn't even hear the rain. Toward nightfall they came across the first of the gold bullion.

"I knew it, I knew it!" shouted Johan and Zandra had to admit this was pretty exciting.

It was soon too dark to carry on. The rain had stopped so Johan took the mules and horses out again. He hooked up the mules and pulled the wagon into the shaft to where the bullion was stacked. He lifted a few bars onto the wagon but decided to leave the rest till the next day. As Zandra had said, they weren't going anywhere for a while. The river was in full flood again.

Zandra grilled a nice lump of ox rump that they had bought in Nelspruit. They had planned to hunt for meat but the rain and the gold had kept them in the cave. The smell of the rump fat dripping into the fire reminded them that they hadn't eaten all day.

After eating, they lay back with their coffee mugs cupped in their hands. Zandra lay back against Johan's chest. He didn't light his pipe, he was thoughtful like that. He was in a good mood and started talking about what they do with the gold.

"We will have to wait some time before we try to sell the gold or people will think that it was us who stole the gold," said Johan.

"I think our only option is to take it to Lorenco Marques," said Zandra.

"But we don't know who to sell it to, well I don't," Johan carried on.

"Someone down at the docks should know," said Zandra, thinking aloud.

"Yes," said Johan getting excited again, "but we will have to hide the wagon until we have a buyer, somewhere in the bush."

After the storm the horses were a bit restless so Johan brought them into the entrance again but they stayed restless in spite of Johan and Zandra gently brushing them. They finally settled and Johan put them right in the entrance so they wouldn't need to keep watch. The two lay together and Zandra started relaxing. They had talked into the late night about what they could do with so much money. They couldn't make up their minds whether they should leave the country or go back to farming on the Flats. They could buy a good breeding stock of cattle and maybe some horses too.

In the early morning light, they realised that they couldn't cross the river yet but if they rode toward Mozambique, they wouldn't need to. Mozambique and Lorenco Marques was in the opposite direction.

Zandra made breakfast of eggs and *mieliemeel* and coffee of course. They were both in a good mood now. Johan busied himself packing the gold to balance the wagon. There was no rope so he had to pack the bullion tight into the corners across the whole width of the wagon.

It was a beautiful sunny morning after she had packed their personal things together, Zandra walked down to the river for the last time. She found the bee-hive where they had taken combs to heal their patients so she took two pieces in a bag to eat on the way. It would give them energy for the long ride.

Johan finished the packing the wagon and started backing the mules toward the entrance. He came around out of the darkness to make sure the path behind the wagon was free. He was looking down at the wheel when a small noise caught his attention. "Nearly ready," he said as he looked up, "we should…..." He never finished speaking.

Standing in front of him with his rifle on his hip was Brand. Johan started bringing his hands up into a surrender position but Brand wasn't taking prisoners. His bullet took Johan through the heart, dead still on his feet. He never did fall down. The bullet went right through, crossed the space behind him and hit the dynamite box on the shelf behind him.

Zandra was coming up the slope in front of the shaft entrance when she heard a crack immediately followed by a boom. The rush of air from the shaft knocked her backwards, off her feet.
She was screaming before she hit the ground, "Johan, Johan, no, no."

She scrambled to her feet and leapt toward the shaft, still screaming. The gasses and dust in the air burnt her throat and lungs as she ran into the shaft. There was so much dust that she couldn't immediately see what had happened. She knew that it was the dynamite but Johan had said that morning that he wouldn't need to use it. As the dust settled, she saw that the wagon had disappeared in the fall of rock.

She screamed and shouted his name but there was no reply. She climbed onto the rocks that had blocked the tunnel but they blocked the whole tunnel all the way to the roof. The mountain shuddered and settled which made her get out as quickly as she could. Half way to her horse she faltered and stopped. The river was too full to cross and the other direction was completely unknown to her. She had heard of a town on the border called Komatipoort but had no idea how to find it. Help was just out of the question. She ran back to the rock-fall but before she got there she knew that she had no hope of reaching Johan. She guessed that he was forward of the wagon and the complete wagon was hidden under the rock.

Zandra sat on the rock for a long time, sobbing. When she looked up it was already dark outside. She unpacked the food stuff and bedding and kept herself busy making herself supper and spreading the bed. For two days she stayed there, waiting for the river to drop again. A number of times she went back to the rock-fall, calling Johan's name but there was no reply. When the river dropped low enough, Zandra packed up again. She was finished crying now, time to go home.

She walked her string of horses across the river bed and up the slope on the other side of the river. She prayed that Johan had died instantly and the mules of course. She had no idea that Brand had died in that shaft and had actually caused the explosion. The shaft looked so peaceful as she turned her horse to look back. The bark of a baboon echoed in the valley. As she swung her horse toward the Flats, she imagined that she heard a horse whinny way to her right but knew there were no other horses around.

As she rode, she wondered if she should swing past Jan and Soekie's place and tell them what had happened to Johan but after a few hours of riding, she decided that some stories should stay untold. It was a long ride home. The nights were especially long and she had to force herself to be strong. Johan's belongings were still in his bags and, for a while, Zandra couldn't bring herself to go through them but eventually she knew it had to be done.

There was a note that he had written, maybe to himself when he thought that there was no one else to talk to. It told how first he was hoping to go back to Soekie but since getting to know Zandra, he only wanted to spend the rest of his life with her. Zandra burnt everything except one shirt which she stuffed into her own bag. Each night she brought it out and put it under her head to sleep on it. She had nightmares of that blast. She didn't know what the crack was before the blast, maybe the detonator. She had never heard dynamite blasting in her life before.

A week later Elsie and Bertus were up and about. They didn't know that Zandra and Johan had gone back to the shaft. They couldn't ride but took the wagon. Even so they had to go slow, scared that the wounds would open as the doctor had warned them. It took them two full days to reach the shaft. The river was down to a small stream again. All the torrents of water hadn't opened the bullion's burial place. The shaft looked the same from the outside. They hadn't seen the mounds of rock of the last resting place of their attackers and they stood, deep in thought looking down on them. They saw the rock-fall in the shaft but didn't know what to make of it.

Well the bullion in the shaft was out of their reach. They were too weak to move any of the rock. Bertus said he thought he could smell a faint aroma of cordite but that could be from all the gun-fire the day of the battle.

The following day they managed to dig four bars out of the river-bed.

"One day we will come back for more," said Bertus, "I need to find out what happened to my friends, why they never came back for their share."

It took both of them to lift the bars onto the wagon, grazing fingers in the process. They spent another day covering the place where they had dug and resting ready for the long ride to Elands River. They found a saddled horse wandering around the bush but not having seen Brand's horse, they didn't know whose horse it was. It seemed to want to stay with them so they took it with them when they left.

The martial eagle watched the two riders with their string of horses. He recognised the gait of the horses that were carrying the riders and knew they belonged to this farm. They were still a long way off so he dropped off the rock, spread his wings and caught a current onto a thermal that took him straight up to hunting level. He wasn't hunting, it was too early in the afternoon. He was curious. The riders came closer. When they came in human eyesight of the farm, the girl shouted and urged her horse into a gallop.

The farmhouse had been rebuilt and there were three horses tethered to the front veranda. The three men had been hard at work these few months since the girl had left. The field to the side had been ploughed and planted and the setting sun would provide a good meal again, either a spring-hare or a grey hare come down to feed on the pea-nuts. They weren't such a mess as a guinea-fowl. A guinea-fowl had to be torn open through the feathers before the entrails could be enjoyed.

The three men came onto the new veranda and then burst into a run toward the girl.

"Pa, Willie, Walter!" the girl shouted, diving off the horse into the old man's arms.

They shouted at each other in pleasure, hugging and squeezing. The man on the other horse following the girl pulled up his horse and waited at a respectable distance until the girl turned and motioned him closer.

THE END

Printed in Poland
by Amazon Fulfillment
Poland Sp. z o.o., Wrocław